In a heated Valentine weekend, Caleb and Jacqueline explore just how far their friendship can go.

Be Mine
By Gwendolyn Cease

Caleb and Jacqueline have been friends for nearly two years since he was engaged to her best friend. But now the engagement is over and Jack wonders where they stand. Jacqueline wants to maintain their friendship, but would prefer so much more.

Caleb invites her to spend Valentine weekend with him at a bed & breakfast since he had made the reservations long before he and Claire broke up. Though the breakup with Claire was only a month ago, the relationship between them had been over long before that. Caleb wants Jacqueline and is prepared to do anything to get her.

And he doesn't just want her for the weekend, he wants her forever. Caleb uses every strategy in his erotic arsenal to convince her she is more than just his friend—she is the woman he loves.

Warning, this title contains explicit sex and graphic language.

A Valentine's date gone wrong marks the beginning of a love that will last for all time.

Forever Valentine
By Bianca D'Arc

Jena knows about vampires, particularly about the one who watches her every step, lest she somehow reveal her knowledge to the mortal world. Ian Sinclair would be her executioner should she even try to share her knowledge, but she doesn't fear him. No, Ian bothers her on an even more elemental level. He's just too sexy for his own good—and hers.

Ian finds himself attracted to the all-too-mortal lady doctor, though he knows better. He's been assigned to watch her, not seduce her, but seduction seems to be all he can think of when he looks at the gorgeous woman who works entirely too hard and has such sad eyes. He feels things he hasn't felt in centuries when she's around, including an unreasonable jealousy when he follows her on a Valentine's date with one of her colleagues.

After the disastrous date, will they both be able to resist temptation when Jena invites the vampire in?

Warning, this title contains explicit sex and graphic language.

Gracie Evans wants a Valentines she won't forget. Luke Forsythe plans to give her exactly what she wants.

Overheard
By Maya Banks

Gracie Evans is a woman tired of the men in her life not satisfying her in bed. She's had a string of boyfriends, but none of them have come close to satisfying the vivid fantasies she has. Two weeks before Valentine's Day, she breaks up with her latest boyfriend after a night of lackluster sex.

When her good friend, Luke Forsythe, overhears her talking to their friend Shelly about what she really wants, he's stunned. And very turned on. Gracie thinks there isn't a man alive who can satisfy her in bed. Luke aims to prove her wrong.

Warning, this title contains explicit sex, graphic language, ménage a trois.

Caught By Cupid

A Samhain Publishing, Ltd. publication.

Samhain Publishing, Ltd.
2932 Ross Clark Circle, #384
Dothan, AL 36301
www.samhainpublishing.com

Caught By Cupid
Print ISBN: 1-59998-345-1
Be Mine Copyright © 2007 by Gwendolyn Cease
Forever Valentine Copyright © 2007 by Bianca D'Arc
Overheard Copyright © 2007 by Maya Banks

Editing by Jessica Bimberg
Cover by Anne Cain

This book is a work of fiction. The names, characters, places, and incidents are products of the writer's imagination or have been used fictitiously and are not to be construed as real. Any resemblance to persons, living or dead, actual events, locale or organizations is entirely coincidental.

All Rights Are Reserved. No part of this book may be used or reproduced in any manner whatsoever without written permission, except in the case of brief quotations embodied in critical articles and reviews.

First Samhain Publishing, Ltd. electronic publication: January 2007
First Samhain Publishing, Ltd. print publication: January 2007

Contents

Be Mine

Gwendolyn Cease

Dedication

To Jess who had enormous faith in me when she called asking me if I wanted to be part of a Valentine anthology. It must be my incredibly fluffy hair and the way I assist in entertaining a whole plane full of people!

To Bianca and Maya—it's been a blast being part of this project with you two. And I'm sure, after everything, Jess still "lurves" us best!

To Sturman, you know why.

Chapter One

Jacqueline Monroe stared out her classroom window at the falling snow. God, she hated February. The holidays were over and the only thing ahead was the huge stretch until April and spring break. She glanced around at her empty room and sighed. She truly should be getting something done while her students were in P.E., but she didn't feel like it. Too many thoughts whirled through her head and none of them school-related.

She absently shoveled through the papers on her desk, stacking and restacking. Who would have known teaching fifth grade meant mountains of paper work? Of course, her students insisted if she gave them less work, she would have less to grade. Yeah, go try that on someone who would listen. She had high expectations for her students and demanded they meet them.

Expectations...she pondered the word. Did she have expectations? She shook her head at the question. Damn, the whole situation with Caleb and Claire had shaken her world. Who would have thought her best friend getting un-engaged would affect her so much? Of course, their pairing had been odd to begin with but things had worked. Or at least they had seemed to. Now who knew what the hell was going on?

Lisa, friend and fellow teacher, stuck her head in the door. "Yo, Jack, what are you doing after school?"

"Is there such a thing as after school?" she replied. "I thought we lived here."

Lisa rolled her eyes. "Yeah, dude, you and me both. I thought since it's Friday we could do chips and salsa."

"I'm there. Regular place at four?"

"You know it. Now I gotta go and express to a snot nose why he must do the work I assigned."

"Good luck," Jacqueline yelled after her.

She and Lisa had become friends the first time they met. Teachers had to stick together and all that, Lisa told her. In actuality, they were the only single women on the faculty and actually had a minute's worth of time. They often spent Friday nights having chips and salsa, code words for drinking lots of margaritas. Right now, she felt like she could use one, two, or maybe ten.

The rest of the day flashed by in a whirl of tests, spelling and math, social studies presentations, and finally end of the day clean-up. By the time her students left, Jack was tired and in deep need of salsa therapy. She looked around at the stack of papers she needed to grade and slowly began to pack it all up. It was either grade here or at home, since not grading was never an option. She found out very quickly, if she missed even one day she was forever trying to play catch-up.

Soon she was sitting in her favorite Mexican restaurant taking the first sip of a mango margarita. She and Lisa munched and drank in silence. Each of them enjoying the knowledge they had two whole days before they had to get back to school. Jack loved to teach. She felt as if she was born to the job, but sometimes she needed a break. And today was one of those times.

"So what's going on?" Lisa asked between sips of her drink.

"Same old shit. The same kid who failed the spelling test on Wednesday failed the make-up today. I keep expressing to him the need to study, but after six months he still isn't getting it."

Lisa laughed. "I didn't mean with school. I was talking about the whole mess with Claire?"

Jack nodded. "She broke her engagement to Caleb about a month ago. Now she's dating a professor she team-teaches with at the university. It looks and sounds serious. I truly think they were kind of looking at each other before she broke it off with Cal. She looks a whole lot happier. I've met him and he's a nice guy. Smart, funny, the whole package."

"How are you and Caleb getting along?"

"We talk about twice a week and have gone out to dinner two or three times. It's awkward at best and weird at worst. Hell, Lisa, she and I met him at the same time. We've known each other for going on two years. The three of us were always doing things together. We went to the movies, dinner, dancing at clubs, and hung out together at Claire's house."

"Yeah, so what's the problem? You two should be getting along fine."

"It's hard to take a relationship with a three person dynamic and all of a sudden cope when there're only two of you. I don't think we quite know where we stand with each other."

"We?" Lisa prompted, popping a chip in her mouth.

"Okay, I don't know where we stand. He's hard to read, you know."

"He's a marine. What do you expect?"

"Ex-marine."

"Yeah, whatever, once a marine always a marine. They may leave the military, but the military doesn't leave them." Lisa took a sip of her drink and grabbed another chip. "So have you tried talking to him?"

"And say what? He was my best friend's fiancé. I don't know what to say to him."

"Hell, he's your friend too. You two need to figure out a relationship alone. You've always told me as we get older we rarely make new friends. We are the exceptions, of course, but then again we are in hell so we must cling together for safety."

Jack laughed. "In hell? You're full of it. You love to teach."

"Yeah, but it would be much better if those kids would leave us alone. We'd get a lot more done."

"That's what I told mine today. Crud on a cracker, people, don't you have somewhere to be? They just laughed."

"The nerve," Lisa finished her drink and waved to the waitress. "Look, call him. Ask him over for dinner. You don't want to lose his friendship."

"You want me to cook him dinner? Ummm, I thought the object was for the two of us to remain friends. Cooking for him would probably chase him away."

Lisa laughed. "There's always take-out."

The two of them moved to other topics as they consumed more chips, salsa and drinks. Jacqueline kept what Lisa had suggested in the back of her mind. Why couldn't she invite him over for dinner? They were friends after all. But the few times they had gone out to dinner she felt odd, like she was somehow cheating on her best friend. She knew this wasn't the case. Claire had already told her time and again she wanted Jack and Caleb to remain friends since they had such a good relationship. Just because Claire and Caleb were no longer engaged didn't mean Jack and Caleb broke up too. Hell, they weren't in grade school. But still the oddness clung. Maybe if she could fully understand why they had broken up it would help. All Claire said was he was too intense and overwhelming for her. She needed someone more laid back.

Soon, Lisa and Jacqueline were paying the bills and heading out to the parking lot. A swift, cold, snowy wind whipped around them, forcing their steps to move more quickly. Jack hugged her coat closer as they hurried to where the cars were parked.

"Call me," Lisa yelled to her. "After you call him, of course, and let me know what he says. Don't wait till Monday."

"Yes, ma'am." Jack smiled and climbed into the freezing interior of her car. She had to get an automatic car starter, she promised herself again. It would be nice to actually walk out to a warm car for a change. She started the car and cranked the heat to its highest setting. The headlights came on for her, a major plus in her book since she frequently forgot to turn them off in her last car. She turned out of the parking lot and headed for home.

The drive was slow going due to the darkness and the snow, but soon she turned into the driveway of her small home. She hurried up the steps and into the warmth. She closed and locked the door behind her, making a mental note to set the alarm before she went to bed. Though the neighborhood was a nice one, she was alone and didn't take chances. She hung her coat up in the closet and headed to her bedroom to change into something more comfortable. Once she was in her favorite pair of sweatpants, she grabbed the heavy shawl her sister had given her for Christmas. She also carried the bags she had brought from school. *Might as well try to get something done tonight.*

She settled on the living room floor and pushed a button on the small remote sitting on the table. The fireplace instantly erupted into a cheerful blaze. There was nothing like a fire on a cold night, especially one she didn't have to do anything to other than push a button. She settled back against the couch and watched the flames. The quiet of the house surrounded her, but for once, it didn't comfort the way it normally did. She rubbed a hand tiredly over her face. It was the weather, she thought, but knew it was a lie. The fact was spending another night alone in her house bothered her.

Instead of pursuing the thought, she grabbed her stereo remote and turned the system on. Sarah McLachlan filled the room with her smooth tone. But still the thoughts wouldn't stop. Here she was, in her early thirties with a wonderful career and great friends. She should be satisfied, but she wasn't. In the deepest part of her heart, she wanted a man to share her life with. Not necessarily marriage, since she had never seen a good one, but someone to love and who loved her in return. People always said she was pretty with her thick dark hair and brown eyes. Her body was tall and lean due to visiting the gym four times a week. On top of all that, she was fun to be around, at least that's what her friends told her. So, what was the deal?

Maybe she was too picky? Her sister said she was, but she should be. Right? Why would she want to spend time with someone because he happened to have a penis? It didn't make sense. She was an educated woman and wanted someone who could carry on an intelligent conversation. Okay, she also wanted a man yummy to look at and awesome in the sex department. But once again, why shouldn't she? Why should sex be a one-way thing? She wanted satisfaction, deep constant satisfaction. It also wouldn't hurt if he had a nice, big—

The chime of the doorbell interrupted her wayward thoughts. Who the hell could be at her door at eight-thirty at night? She jumped up and hurried to the door, pulling her shawl closer around her shoulders. Flipping on the front light, she looked out the window to find Caleb Sinclair standing on her front porch. What the hell? It was as if thinking about him all day had conjured him up.

Slowly, she unlocked the door and opened it. He watched her closely with deep whiskey-colored eyes. They looked at one another until Jack blinked and broke whatever weirdness had a hold of her.

"Caleb, what's going on?" Her voice sounded husky and a bit uncertain even to her own ears. "Are you okay?"

"Can I come in?"

She moved aside to allow him to enter her house, feeling the whole time things were changing. She wasn't sure if she was quite ready for whatever was heading her way.

Chapter Two

Caleb Sinclair was a big man, not only in height, but in breadth too. He topped nearly six-two with shoulders so broad a friend had once remarked she bet he could put a house on his shoulder and move it. Dark brown hair shot with sunlight was still cut military short to tame the curls, which made an appearance if he let it get too long. His face was angular and chiseled, more arresting than handsome. He would never be a pretty boy, but he always stood out in a crowd.

Jacqueline followed him into her living room. He had been to her house plenty of times with Claire, but never on his own. She watched as he paced about, his energy barely leashed. This was a man used to action. Since leaving the military, he had put his talents into starting a security company with a friend. Thankfully, Jason was much better suited to sit behind a desk taking care of the daily running of the office. If Caleb had been forced to take over the role, he would have quickly gone insane.

"Do you want something to drink?" Jack asked as she headed to the kitchen. Her home wasn't large, but the fireplace and the spacious kitchen more than made up for it. Unfortunately, Jack didn't take as much advantage of the kitchen as she should, but it was home and warm on a cold winter evening.

He followed her, still not speaking, and leaned against the counter, watching her move about. His jeans and boots told her he had gotten off work early, since he wore dress clothes to visit clients. But nothing explained why he was standing in her home late on a Friday evening. She knew he had begun to date since the breakup so it had to be something important to drive him to her small home.

She looked up to find him watching her intently. "What?"

He shook his head. "You look tired. Are you okay?"

She laughed. "Wow, a man comes into my home and tells me I look bad after I offered him hospitality. With skills like that, Sinclair, I bet the women are falling all over you."

He burst out laughing. "I didn't mean for it to come out as an insult, Jacqueline. You know that."

"I know, but someone has to give you a hard time. What's up?"

"I wanted to stop by and see how you're doing." He accepted the cup of coffee she handed him.

"I'm okay. Tired—as you kindly pointed out. School is going well, but I hate this time of year."

"I know what you mean. The holidays were great, but now nothing."

"At least I have spring break to look forward to," she replied, leading him back into the living room where the fire created a cozy tableau. She took a seat on the couch, still not certain why he had come over. Caleb never did anything on the spur of the moment. Everything was always well thought out and planned. His small security company was a sure success because of this trait.

He sat close beside her on the couch and placed his cup on the small table. She watched him and wondered what was going on. She hated to be off kilter in situations. But without some kind of clue, she was walking blind.

"I did have a reason for stopping by without calling." He turned to look at her. "What are you doing next weekend for Valentine's Day?"

"Well, Hugh Jackman called me and wants me to fly to New York to be with him," Jack joked. "I told him I would have to get back with him because I might have something important to do like get my nails done or wash my hair." At his look, she smiled. "Not a damn thing. I'm off on Friday because it's a professional development day. Thankfully, since I've already been developed professionally this year, I have the day off. I'll probably spend the weekend getting caught up on grading and complete my lesson plans for the following week. Why? What are you doing?"

"I was hoping you would go with me."

"Go with you? Where?"

"There's this bed and breakfast Claire went on and on about. It has this small cottage behind the main house, and she was all excited. I made reservation at the end of the summer, you know, as a surprise. Now, I have the place reserved from Thursday evening to Sunday..." He trailed off.

"And what?" Jacqueline asked, unsure of where the conversation was headed. "I don't understand."

"Yeah, I'm not making myself real clear." He leaned forward to place his hand on her knee. "I want you to go with me."

"Me?" She was stunned. What the hell? Why would he ask her?

"Yeah, you. Jacqueline, you and I have been friends for going on two years now. Just because Claire and I broke up doesn't mean we need to do the same. I think this might be a nice way to build our own relationship. We can spend some time together without the day-to-day shit." He reached in his pocket and pulled out a brochure. "Why don't you look this over and let me know. The town it's in is small, but the place sits right on a lake. They even serve tea, which I know you're into. Think about it. If you agree, we can leave as soon as you get out of school on Thursday. It only takes a couple hours so we should be there around six."

Jacqueline took the brochure from him. The picture on the front showed a beautiful home with the name Willow Creek underneath. She knew this place. She and Claire discovered the website for it and instantly fell in love. Claire must have mentioned the place to Caleb, hoping he would take the hint. Obviously, he had. Only now, Claire wouldn't be the one going, Jacqueline would. If she agreed.

"I'd like to think about it, okay?" She finally looked up to find him watching her.

"Call me on my cell." He stood and took his cup into the kitchen. "I'd better go. I told Jason I'd meet him to go over a bid we're working on for an office building."

Jack walked him to the door and opened it to the still falling snow. "Be careful. The weather guy says the snow's going to stop, but he missed the ten inches at Christmas too."

"I will." He leaned over to brush his lips against her cheek. "Call me."

Jacqueline closed and locked the door behind him. She sagged against it in disbelief. Oh my gosh, Caleb had asked her to go away with him for the weekend. Shivers ran up her spine before she could clamp down on her emotions. As friends, she told herself. They were going because he had the reservations and didn't want to waste them. *Why not give them to someone else,* a little voice whispered.

"Because everyone probably already had plans," she spoke aloud. She walked over to the couch and picked up the brochure. Sitting, she began to look through it. The cottage, where he had the reservations, looked to be a house in miniature. It had a living room, bedroom, large bath and tiny kitchen. More than enough room for the two of them to stay there comfortably. The brochure even made mention of the couch rolling out to a bed. Each of them would have someplace to sleep without bothering the other.

Bothering? The tiny voice was back. *You'd love if he bothered you. Bothered you right out of your clothes and right into bed.* Jacqueline shoved those thoughts aside and began to reason as she always did.

"Caleb is a handsome man, at least I think he is. He's got an amazing body and even better personality. Of course, you would be attracted to him. You'd have to be dead not to. But he's a friend."

But why, the voice asked. *He's not engaged to Claire anymore. Why does he have to be only a friend? Why can't he be the kind of friend you take your clothes off with? The kind of friend who licks your—*

"No!" She stood up and hurried to the kitchen, pretending to clean up. "Besides what would he want with me? I mean, hells bells, I'm not tiny, cute and blonde. That's what he goes for. If you need any better example look at Claire. Look at the girls he's dated since breaking up with Claire. All of them have been petite, blond and cute as hell."

She looked at herself in the mirror to find tall, dark and wouldn't be petite if you paid someone. She laughed out loud. Now that the Friday night tequila insanity was over, she would sit and grade. It did no good to create fantasies around Caleb Sinclair. He was a friend. Tucking the thoughts away, Jack went back into the living room and pulled out her grade book. Way less fun, but definitely safer.

Caleb sat in his car staring at the dimly lit house. Fuck, his life was a mess. First, his engagement to Claire had been broken, which he didn't feel as bad about as he felt he should. Now he was inviting a friend to spend the weekend at a bed and breakfast. If he were smart, he would invite Stephie or whatever the hell her name was. But no, he had to go and ask Jacqueline. What the fuck had he been thinking? There was only one answer. He hadn't been. Or at least not with his mind. His cock twitched in his jeans. He wanted her. The breakup with Claire had only made it more obvious. Did she want him? He shook his head; he knew he was going to try to find out. No matter what he told himself, he would. He wanted Jacqueline spread out before him. Naked and submissive, open to his every whim. He shook the thought away. He had to get a hold of himself. What if she didn't agree? He clenched his teeth. She would, she had too. If she didn't, he knew he could convince her. Or die trying. Either way she would be going with him to the fucking bed and breakfast one way or the other.

Chapter Three

“He did what?” Lisa demanded on the phone the next day.

“He asked me to go to a bed and breakfast with him next weekend.” Jack’s voice came out sounding calm, but inside she was far from it. The whole idea of spending three nights alone with Caleb had brought dreams hot enough to scorch the sheets. She had awakened multiple times during the night, sweating, with the sheets wrapped around her as if she had been thrashing about. Yeah, if her sleep was anything like the dreams she was surprised she hadn’t fallen right out of bed. “He said it would give us time to talk. Build a relationship of our own.”

“Yeah, I bet he wants to build a relationship. The kind where you both strip and fuck like rabbits.”

Jack laughed. “Lisa, that is not what he wants.”

“Dude, who are you kidding? Why else would he ask you to go away for the weekend? To a bed and breakfast? To the honeymoon cottage?”

“He made the reservations ages ago and, I’m sure, doesn’t want to lose the money. It wasn’t cheap from what I remember of the prices.”

"Jacqueline, I've been to Willow Creek. The cottage in the back is referred to as the honeymoon cottage since it's private. The bed in it is enormous. Don't tell me he isn't planning on putting it to use and you aren't willing."

Jack slumped low in a chair and stared out the window at the small flakes still falling from the sky. Leave it to Lisa to put everything right on out there. Could she deny she wanted him? Hell no. But did he want her? She highly doubted it. "Okay, I'll admit I'd jump his bones in a heartbeat, but there is no reciprocal jumping from him. He isn't interested. And even if he were, I'm sure it would be because he hasn't had sex in a while. And I'll be damned if I'm going to be fucked just because I'm convenient."

"Why not?" Lisa demanded, her voice loud through the phone. "If he's willing, take him up on it. Damn, girl, you need to get laid. And from what you've said, he is hot."

"He is," she agreed. "But I don't want to mess up a friendship for sex. And if that's all he's interested in, I guess I wouldn't want him for a friend anyway."

"Have you ever thought he might be attracted to you? Since you have such a good relationship he wants to turn up the heat?"

Jack laughed softly. "Lisa, I am so not his type. I've already told you."

"I know, petite, blonde and cute. But it's obviously not working for him, maybe he thinks tall, leggy and brunette would be much better. Look, don't say anything. Think about it and call him to say you'll go. If nothing else you'll get a nice long weekend getaway without having to pay. And you know we teachers need all the fun we can get, especially with as long as it is 'til spring break."

"I'll think about it."

"Yeah, and once you do, call him and accept. You'll kick yourself if you don't."

Jacqueline busied around her house the rest of the day. She did the much dreaded bathroom cleaning, changed the sheets on her bed and got laundry started. Since she was feeling in an industrious mood, she vacuumed her bedroom carpet and swept the hardwood floors. She polished and rearranged her kitchen cabinets, and finally cleaned out the refrigerator. Slumping exhausted in a chair, she had to admit she was putting the phone call off. A huge part of her wanted to call and accept, but the smaller and more rational part knew she shouldn't. She just didn't want to take the chance of getting hurt.

But, she argued to herself, *if I don't take chances, how will I get anywhere*? Teaching was a huge chance. At the age of thirty-one, she had come to the realization she wanted to teach so she had begun to take classes toward her master's degree in teaching. After the long struggle of school, unemployment due to student teaching and the general stress of everyday life, she had finally fulfilled her dream. At thirty-three, she was teaching fifth grade in a school she loved. She couldn't imagine her life any other way.

Was this time any different? She looked around her small living room without seeing it. She knew whatever she decided to do she had to talk to Claire first. She had been engaged to the man for over a year, so if Jack was even briefly thinking about doing things with Caleb involving nakidity, she needed to talk to her best friend. Did she want Claire to talk her out of it? Or even more demand she not see him? Jack burst out laughing. This was not a soap opera and they weren't school kids. She knew neither one of those choices would happen. But she still knew she needed to talk to Claire.

"Jacqueline," Claire hugged her enthusiastically. "Come in. Does this weather suck or what?"

Jack laughed, following her best friend into her comfortable two-bedroom condo. Claire had declared early in her house search that she would be damned if she did yard work. Once she had set eyes on the condo, it had become home instantly. Jack didn't know how she stood having people live all around her in such close quarters, but Claire had told her they were old and couldn't hear much anyway.

Claire Fielding was a petite five-four, though she claimed five-five since she was sure her hair gave her the extra height. Her blonde shoulder-length mane flowed into soft natural waves, which Jack knew she didn't do a thing to in the morning. Claire's green eyes were fringed with lashes of softest gold, and even in February's cold, her skin was smooth and nearly flawless. All in all, if she weren't her best friend Jacqueline was sure she could very easily hate Claire. Or probably not, since Claire was oblivious to her looks, kind and giving to a fault. Sometimes she wanted to make Jack toss her cookies.

"What brings you out today?" Claire led the way to her small kitchen and pulled out a kettle to begin heating water for tea. "I thought you were going to grade all weekend?"

"I was, but something kind of came up." Jack opened a cabinet and found cups and saucers. She looked over Claire's small loose-leaf tea collection and chose the China Rose Petal. "Man, I am going to have to get you more tea."

Claire laughed. "You say the same thing every time you see my tiny stash. Actually, I ordered some from the online place you told me about. Now that I've had loose leaf, I can't go back. Does it mean I'm a tea snob too?"

"Well, you know you've reached the snob level when you go to a tea place and make a face if it's bag. Once you make the face, you create your own tea kit and carry it everywhere you go."

"Like you do."

"Exactly." She pulled a teapot from the cabinet. "I can't stand bag tea now. It's nasty and bitter." Jacqueline pulled an exaggerated face. "Oh my, I'm letting my snobbishness out."

Both women laughed as they moved through the ritual of making tea. Soon they were seated at the cozy kitchen table silently sipping the smooth lightly flavored beverage. Jacqueline could feel her worries slide away as she and her best friend sat, as they had dozens of times, and enjoyed the silence. The only sounds she could hear were the ticking of the clock and the rush of wind against the windows.

"What's going on?" Claire broke the silence. "You said something came up."

"Caleb came to see me last night."

"How's he doing?"

Jack watched her best friend closely, but could see nothing that screamed out Claire still loved him. Even though she was the one to break the engagement, Jack often wondered if she regretted it now. But Claire was as open as she had always been, and they'd known each other far too long to lie to each other.

"He's busy. The security company's taking off and he works all the time."

"That's great. But it's not the reason you came over here, is it?"

"Claire, Caleb asked me to go away with him next weekend. As friends," she rushed to explain. "He made some reservations and instead of losing them he thought he and I could go and spend some time together. You know, as friends."

Claire smiled. "Jack, even if you and Cal weren't going as friends, it's okay with me. Our engagement is over. I'm seeing Dan now and our relationship is good. Really good, in fact."

Jack sipped her tea. "I needed you to know about this from me, since I didn't want you to hear it from someone else. But I still don't think it's any big deal. He said we could use the time to reconnect. Our relationship has been odd since the two of you broke it off. I'm sure there's nothing more to it."

"Don't be too sure." Claire shook her head. "Caleb always did think you were very attractive. He always wanted to know why a beautiful woman like you wasn't seeing anyone serious."

"He said that?" Jacqueline was stunned. "Whatever, it still doesn't mean he's attracted to me. And it doesn't mean I'm attracted to him."

"I don't want you to get hurt." Claire's face took on a serious cast. "You know I didn't talk much about the private stuff between me and Caleb."

"Yeah, since you and I both get totally grossed out when people talk about their sex lives. Absolute TMI to the extreme."

"Well for once I'm going to break the rule since I want you to know what you're getting into. First, Cal is a big guy. All over." Claire rolled her eyes as Jack laughed. "Yeah, you get the picture. Believe me, the first time I saw him nude my jaw dropped and all I could think was *there is no way, he is never gonna fit.* Anyway, he was patient and tender, but the sex was never good for me. It felt more like he was going through the motions than making love to me. I mean I had orgasms, don't get me wrong, he made sure of it. But it wasn't all I thought it should be.

"I had a feeling he was holding himself back from me. I don't know for sure, since he didn't want to talk about bedroom issues, but it's the impression I got."

Jacqueline leaned back in her chair watching her best friend. The only thought floating through her mind was just how big was *big*? She brought herself back to the conversation with a shake. "What about Dan?"

Claire laughed. "Totally different. Dan is a more manageable size and he's very enthusiastic. Man, he can push my buttons. He reminds me of the guy you dated...Tom?"

"Tim," she supplied.

"Right him. Dan reminds me of him. You know, gentle and loving. He touches me, wow, like I'm precious. And we always have a good time, even during sex. Sometimes we laugh so hard we can hardly do anything."

"You sound like you love him."

"I think I do." Claire poured more tea in her cup. "He's open with me, talks to me. Sometimes with Caleb, I didn't know where I stood. He's serious, too serious for me. And like I said, the sex wasn't too enjoyable. The first time we were together it was intense, scary even."

"What do you mean?"

"He, umm, gosh...he's so big, I felt crushed and he talked to me the whole time. Really, dirty talk that didn't turn me on at all. I finally asked him to stop, which he did right away. The silence, though, was even worse." Claire put her cup down and stared at Jacqueline. "Jack, he's not like anyone either one of us has dated before. I mean, I don't know for sure, but I listened to some of his friends talk and I think his sexual practices were a little extreme before me."

"Extreme? I don't get it. Does he like to dress in women's clothes?"

Both girls burst out laughing at the thought of Caleb—all six-foot-two of him—stuffed in a dress. Claire wiped her eyes, shaking her head. "No, you goof. I think he was maybe into more domination games. I don't know for sure. I mean I'm drawing a conclusion from stuff they said. Hell, they could have been making shit up to scare me too. All I want for you to do is be careful. I don't want you hurt."

Jacqueline drove home with all the things Claire had said spinning through her mind. She clenched her thighs together at the sensation of moisture pooling between her legs. The good girl teacher part of her thought the things Claire told her should send her running and screaming. The other half, the much bigger half, wanted to scream too, but running from him wasn't part of the equation. She again wondered how big, big was. Claire was nearly a foot shorter than Caleb, so the difference between them was pretty extreme. Jack, at five-nine, was only five inches shorter and she certainly was not petite.

Fuck, why was she even thinking about this? For all she knew they were going to spend time together as friends. She would hate to build herself up for something great and have nothing happen. But still she couldn't keep her thoughts from moving back to what Claire had said. Tim, the man who Claire brought up, had been a short-lived relationship Jack was more than glad to see gone. Since she and Claire never talked about their sex lives, her friend didn't know the particulars about the relationship. When she thought of Tim the word association she had was "boring", with a huge capital B. The sex had been even worse. At least Caleb had made sure Claire had an orgasm. Tim couldn't find one with a road map and a compass.

Jacqueline had really tried too, but the longer the relationship went on the more dissatisfied she had become. Pretty soon, she began to truly hate when Tim called. When those feelings surfaced, she broke the relationship off. Better to spend Friday evenings alone then to have to sneak into the bathroom and masturbate after sex. The saddest part was Tim never even realized she hadn't had an orgasm. Or, most probably, he didn't care one way or the other. As for oral sex, he loved it when she went down on him. But the one time he had reciprocated, he was tentative and truly grossed out by the act. She had finally made him stop after only a minute. Damn, men were such dicks.

She turned into her driveway and shut the car off. She sat watching small snowflakes gently touch the window and melt quickly away. Her house sat before her dark and empty, while the others in the neighborhood had actually put up Valentine's Day lights and decorations. Valentine's Day. Did she want to spend another one alone? Jacqueline realized she had already made up her mind. In fact, it had been made up before she and Claire had finished talking. She would go away with Caleb for the weekend. And, if he made moves acting as if he wanted her, she would move right back. Hell, what did she have to lose?

Caleb snapped his cell phone shut, smiling. Jacqueline had finally called and agreed to go with him. The rush of pleasure he got from hearing her voice had intensified when she told him she would go to the B&B. He sat back in his chair and twirled the phone absently in his hand. He had to make plans. He wanted the weekend to be great. He had to get wine for her, since she liked the stuff, beer for himself, maybe some snacking kind of foods, and flowers. Definitely had to get her some flowers. It was Valentine's Day after all, and a beautiful woman like Jacqueline deserved them. Roses, maybe, but not in a vase. Something more, something special.

"What's going on?" Jason, his partner and friend, cut into his thoughts.

"That was Jacqueline. She said she'd go with me next weekend."

Jason eyed him from across the office they shared. "Cal, do you know what you're doing? She's your ex-fiancée's best friend and you're inviting her to go away for the weekend with you. Buddy, you need to get over Claire and move on. Look, I know this girl named Debbie, I think you'll flip over her. Blonde, hot, built like a brick shithouse and a total freak in bed."

Caleb shook his head. "No thanks. I'm not interested."

"Not interested? In sex? With a totally hot babe? Come on, let me tell you she can suck your lungs right out your dick and you won't mind it a bit."

Cal gave a small laugh. "Jason, I'm interested in sex, but not with the blonde vacuum cleaner."

"Bud, Claire broke up with you. It's over. You need to quit thinking about her and move on."

He shook his head. "None of this has anything to do with Claire. I'm over her. Hell, I was probably over her before she broke the engagement."

"What's the deal?"

Caleb didn't answer. *What was the deal?* Before he would have loved to go out with Jason's blonde. Hell, he would have loved fucking the blonde, but now it didn't even appeal. The only person he could think about was Jacqueline. Jacqueline with the thick brunette hair, long legs and fantastic tits. Jacqueline of the quirky sense of humor and gentle personality. God, he couldn't stop thinking about her. Couldn't stop wanting her. And none of it had to do with Claire and everything to do with Jacqueline.

"Damn, you have it bad." Jason broke through his thoughts. "Don't you think getting involved with her is a bad idea?"

Slowly, he shook his head. "No, it might be one of the best I've had. Either way I'm going to find out."

"Man, I hope you don't regret it."

"I won't," Caleb said with certainty. "The only thing I'd regret is not going. And no matter what, Jacqueline and I are both going to be at the B&B at the end of the week. And I plan on us having a weekend neither one will forget."

Chapter Four

By Thursday, Jack felt as if she had been strung up and left to die. She had promptly called Caleb and accepted his invitation after her conversation with Claire. Now, she was having second thoughts. Screw second thoughts, tenth or fifteenth thoughts. At least four times a day she reached for the phone to call him and cancel. But something or someone always stopped her. She couldn't back out now since he was coming to pick her up right after school. She had even tried leaving a message for him on his voice mail, but he had never called her back. Part of her was thankful, but the other half wanted to whimper and hide.

"How are you doing?" Lisa stuck her head in as the last student left the room.

"Can I say how quickly this week went?" Jack tried to smile, but failed miserably. "Am I out of my fucking mind? I must have been smoking crack when I told him I would go with him. I have a lot to do this weekend. I can't go running off and play at some bed and breakfast."

"If you're trying out the arguments you're going to use on him, they're crappy lame. In fact, they suck out loud."

"Really? I thought they sounded pretty good." She slid lower in her chair.

Lisa sat on her desk and smiled. "Look, nothing can happen unless you want it to. Jack, you've known him for about two years. If he was some crazed rapist I'm sure you would have figured it out by now. Since he's not, whatever happens or doesn't happen is totally up to you. Personally, girl, I'd grab that stallion and ride him."

Jack shook her head in wonder. "Where the hell do you get this shit?"

"I don't know. I make it up. I'm thinking of putting it on a bumper sticker, what do you think?"

"I think you're on crack too."

Lisa burst out laughing. "No, but I will be on chips and salsa as soon as the day is done. And you, my lucky friend, will be on her way to a wonderful place with a hunk. Don't let him go to waste. Put him to work for you. He'll never need batteries and you won't have to charge him."

"Great, thanks for the shit advice. At least with the battery-operated deal you don't have to have a conversation."

"Who said you had to have one with this guy? All you have to do is nod every so often. Boys don't care, they mostly like to hear themselves talk."

Before Jacqueline could reply the phone in her classroom rang. She picked it up and was told she had a visitor in the office. As she hung up, she could feel her palms get sweaty and her stomach roll and pitch. She couldn't do this. She would go down and tell him she couldn't go. Something with a student had come up and she had to cancel.

"If you think of skipping out on him, I will hound you till you die. Then I'll tell him you're a big fat lying head," Lisa warned her. "Now get your shit together and get downstairs."

Jack nodded and slowly began to gather her things. Locking her classroom, she and Lisa went down the stairs. As they reached the bottom, she could see Caleb standing in the office. Damn, he looked way good. He was dressed casually in jeans and an old leather jacket, which had seen better days. He was talking on his cell phone and didn't see their approach. She was able to watch without him noticing and, wow, was the view great. He stood with one hand in the pocket of his jeans, which pulled the material taut across his butt. And did he have a good one.

"He is hot," Lisa whispered. "You'd be a fool to even think of not going with him. And, girl, if he wants to get naked, get your clothes off. He looks like he would be well worth the effort."

He turned to face the girls, like he sensed he was being watched. A slow smile spread over his face and Jacqueline answered with a smile of her own. As if his smile fixed something, Jack was glad she had accepted his invitation. Here was Caleb, her friend. The friend who had laughed and talked with her and even brought her soup when she had been sick. He hadn't been her friend only because of his engagement to Claire. They were friends because they got along and had fun together.

"Have a good time." Lisa nudged her. "Remember what I told you."

"I will."

Lisa hurried off to her classroom as Caleb came out of the office toward her. Wow, he looked even better close up. But he always had.

Caleb walked out of the office toward Jacqueline. Damn, she looked good enough to eat. She was all dressed in her conservative teacher wear and he wondered what she had on under it. He knew she had a thing for pretty lingerie, since she and Claire were always going through catalogs and ordering online. Unlike Claire's petite build, Jacqueline was lush and athletic. Even engaged, he had noticed how beautiful she was. Hell, he had been engaged not dead. And a guy would have to be dead to not notice Jacqueline. He always wondered why she didn't have a boyfriend, but was glad now she didn't. He'd hate to have to scare someone off, but now he didn't have to. He would have her all to himself the whole weekend.

"How are you doing?" He hugged her close. "Ready to go?"

"I'm good. I need to sign out and get my things."

He kept a possessive hand on her waist as he followed her back to the office. Once he touched her, he didn't want to stop. He knew she had called earlier and he had purposely ignored the call since he was almost positive she was going to try and back out. No matter what, he wasn't going to let it happen. He was getting her to go with him if he had to tie her up and carry her. The thought of Jacqueline tied naked to a bed made him instantly hard. He wanted her and he was going to do whatever was necessary to convince her of the same.

Jacqueline disappeared into the back offices and reappeared in moments wearing her coat and carrying a small suitcase. Caleb stepped forward to relieve her of it and waited while she wished everyone a great weekend. Soon they were tucked into his SUV and headed out of the parking lot. She sat quietly beside him and he decided not to press her for conversation. He wanted her to get used to the two of them being alone together. The sooner they were comfortable, the better things would go. And he did want her to enjoy the weekend.

He thought back to the conversation he had with Jason before he left the office. The whole idea of hanging out with Jack to be close to Claire had made him sick. Who would not want Jacqueline? She was a sexy, beautiful woman. Even if the men in her life before didn't realize it. Better for him, they didn't. He and Claire were long over. Fuck, they had been over before she had broken the engagement. He knew they had both realized it too. But for some reason they held on, probably because it was comfortable for both of them more than anything. He had been more than a bit relieved when she finally gave him the ring back and called it quits.

"You called me today." He finally broke the silence. "I'm sorry I didn't get a chance to call you back. I was trying to get everything squared away before we left. I didn't want Jason to have any reason to call me while we were gone." He glanced over at her, wondering if she would tell the truth or fib. But Jack was honest to a fault, as she often reminded him. Don't ask her opinion unless you want it.

"I'm glad you didn't. I was going to tell you I couldn't go."

"Why?"

She shrugged. "You and I have been friends for almost two years. But it was always a three-way relationship. Being alone with you… I don't know. I guess I was worried we wouldn't have anything to talk about. You know, like suddenly we'd have nothing in common."

He laughed. "Jacqueline, you and I have never lacked for conversation. Claire often said we sometimes didn't even realize she had left the room we were so busy talking."

"Arguing?" she supplied with a smile.

"That too, you and I differ on some of our opinions. I don't think either of us will find ourselves sitting in silence for long."

Once the ice had been broken, conversation flowed easily. Caleb relaxed as he and Jacqueline settled back into a normal rhythm. They talked on topics as diverse as politics and religion. Eventually, the talk moved to her teaching and his company. As she spoke, Caleb found himself actually smiling for no reason other than they were together. He hoped the rest of the weekend went as well or better. Especially since he wanted to do a whole lot more with her than sit and talk. He wanted Jacqueline, and as the miles sped by, he found he could very easily picture her spread naked on the bed under him. He shoved those images aside for now. He didn't need to get into a wreck because he couldn't keep his mind on the road. For now, he would ease back and let things go at their own pace. They had plenty of time for other things later.

Jack wondered for the twelfth time what she had been worrying about. Initially, the trip had been awkward, but once they started talking she forgot all about the worries. She and Caleb were on a trip. Two friends on a trip. Friends? Once again, the question came up—did she want her relationship with Caleb to be only friendly? And once again, she wasn't sure of the answer. After the conversation with Claire, she knew she wanted him even more. Did Claire exaggerate about his size? Jack highly doubted it, since her friend was a real no nonsense type. And she knew as long as they had been friends they had never lied to one another. There wasn't a reason. They were both no bullshit kind of people, honest to the point of extreme.

Jack smiled thinking back to a night not too long ago when she and Claire were getting ready to go out. Claire had come out of her bedroom wearing jeans and a pair of boots. She had spun in front of Jacqueline and asked her what she thought. Jack, as always, did not hold back one bit.

"Those pants make your ass look huge."

"You're kidding." Claire turned as if to see her own butt.

"Nope, it looks about this big." She held her hands up to show an impossibly large measure.

"Well, fuck, I guess I'll throw these pants out." Back she had gone to change into a skirt, which Jack told her looked awesome.

But if she tried her deadly honesty on Caleb would he appreciate it? Hell, she wasn't even sure she wanted to. She almost laughed at her indecision. This had never happened to her before. She usually made up her mind quickly and jumped right in. Figuring out the situation was giving her a headache. She decided to let things go without any planning. If sex did somehow come up, which she doubted it would, she'd make the decision in the moment. It was ridiculous to try to plan for something that may or may not happen.

Caleb pulled the vehicle into the small parking area of Willow Creek. It was later than he had planned on arriving, but he and Jack had been having so much fun at dinner the time had flown. He glanced at his watch—nearly eight. He hoped someone would be up to take care of them, since bed and breakfasts were nothing like the hotels he was used to staying in.

"Don't move," he told her as he exited the vehicle. He came around to her side and opened the door. Normally, she moved so quickly he didn't have a chance to give her the courtesy.

"Thanks," she smiled. "You didn't have to get my door."

"Yes, I did." He pulled their bags from the back. "I know you're used to doing things on your own, but I want to at least attempt to be a gentleman."

She laughed. "Fair enough. And thank you."

He locked the car and ushered her to the well-lit front porch. The home was grand with a wrap-around porch large enough to hold chairs and tables in warmer weather. Maybe if they had a good time they could come back again. Caleb was going to do his best to convince her anyway. He still wasn't sure what was going on, but ever since the broken engagement—shit, he had to admit, before it—he enjoyed spending time with Jacqueline. But since the engagement was over, he had spent more time thinking about her. Wanting her. He didn't want to fuck up their friendship, but damn he had it bad. He not only wanted her naked; he wanted her subject to his every whim. He wanted her to scream while he ate her out. He wanted to watch her take his dick in her mouth and suck it like her favorite watermelon Popsicle.

He kept her in front of him as his jeans got tighter. Shit, he had to get his mind out of the gutter, at least until they got to the room. Wouldn't do for the whole world to see his hard on, especially the nice lady he talked to on the phone. He opened the door and allowed Jacqueline to enter first. The entry was spacious with a flight of stairs to the left and a modest desk to the right. A woman who looked to be in her early fifties waited for them with a smile on her face.

"Welcome, welcome to Willow Creek. I'm Amanda Hayden. You must be the Sinclairs. I got worried when you weren't here an hour ago."

"We stopped for dinner and lost track of time," Cal told her as he placed the luggage at his feet.

"As long as nothing bad happened. The weather this time of year is tricky. Oh heavens," she fluttered about, "I'm sure you don't want to stand here talking with me. Let me get your signature and I'll show you to the cottage."

Cal quickly signed the guest book and took the key. "Why don't you tell us where we need to go? I'd hate for you to have to come back here in the dark."

The woman hesitated. "Well, if you're sure it would be okay?"

Jacqueline spoke up. “Of course it’s okay. Who’d want to go out in the cold if you didn’t have to? We’ll be fine.”

“You two are so sweet.” She led them through a large dining room to a small side door. “This is your entrance since you’re staying in our cottage. Breakfast is served at nine-thirty and is quite good, if I do say so myself. Everything you need is in the cottage and if not, dial zero to ring me on the phone.

“All you need to do is go down the side steps and follow the walkway around to the back. Go through a gate and it will lead you right to your front door. You two have a wonderful stay.”

Caleb and Jacqueline thanked her as they went back out into the cold. He kept close to her as they walked a well-lit path through the trees. In the spring, he imagined, it was probably beautiful. Now it was dark and cold. Finally, they reached a small green garden gate, which Jack opened. Before them on the path was the cottage. It was already lit and looked warm and cozy. He couldn’t see much in the darkness, but thought it was probably what his mother always called quaint. He hoped like hell it was as warm as it looked. When the sun went, the tiny bit of warmth the day held did too. It was now bone-chillingly cold.

Jacqueline’s teeth chattered as he opened the door and let her go in first. The warmth of a small living room greeted them and he heard her sigh. That one sound made his cock hard again. Damn, if he didn’t watch out, he’d end up coming in his pants, which hadn’t happened since he was twelve looking through his father’s *Playboy* magazines.

The living room held a large couch he knew rolled out to a bed and two plush chairs. A television sat tucked into a rustic entertainment center, which also held a small stereo. Through a set of French doors was the only bedroom. A massive four-poster bed of rich dark wood dominated the room, set against a creamy yellow wall. A huge fireplace dominated the wall across from the bed, and he could tell right away it was gas. There would be no messing with wood and matches on this trip. The floor was hardwood, but had thick throw rugs to comfort feet on a cold morning. A large wardrobe and two nightstands completed the room. The only thing missing was the view from the floor to ceiling windows. He knew from talking to the owner they would have an unhampered view of the lake. Since it was February, heavy burgundy drapes were drawn tight against the cold.

"This is nice." Jacqueline wandered around the room checking things out. She opened a closed door to reveal the master bath. "Okay, I take it back. This is fantastic. The bathroom is spectacular." She ended her observation with a yawn. "Sorry."

"Don't apologize, babe. It's been a long day. Why don't you take a shower and get comfortable. I'm going to go back out to the truck and bring the food in I brought."

"You brought food too? You should have said something. I would have gotten us stuff."

"Jacqueline, this is my treat remember?"

She nodded. "At least let me help you get everything in."

"No way. Go in and relax. You've already been out in the cold enough. Your teeth were chattering. Climb in a hot shower and unwind."

She opened her mouth to argue, but smiled instead. "Okay, if you insist."

"I do."

She grabbed her bag and headed to the bathroom, shutting the door behind her. Caleb started the trip back outside to the SUV. He needed the cold air to cool down, he wanted to be able to take things slow. He did not want to end up jumping on her like some jackass.

Jack climbed under steaming, hot water. It felt like complete heaven. She dropped her head fall forward and let the water beat at the base of her neck. She had taken something for the tension headache she'd had all week. She hoped the damn thing went away now they were here. She admitted to herself, she was having a good time. She had forgotten how much fun she and Caleb had together. They'd always had an easy relationship and spending time with him reminded her of the fact.

She showered before leaving for school, so she quickly turned off the water and climbed out. Truthfully, the reason was she wanted to be out of the shower and in her pajamas when she saw him again. She dried off and rubbed her favorite lotion on all the exposed skin she could reach. She hated winter and one of the huge reasons was if she didn't apply the stuff every day she would flake away to nothing.

She pulled on one of her favorite jammy sets and exited the bathroom. The cottage was quiet and she assumed he was still out getting the stuff together. She wondered briefly what he had brought, but figured she could check it all out when he came back in. Grabbing a teaching magazine out of her bag, she climbed on the bed. She shoved some pillows up and laid back. The bed was as comfortable as it looked. She smiled as she opened the magazine and began to read.

Caleb shut the door of the quiet cottage. He had gotten waylaid by a call from Jason as he was bringing all the stuff in and knew he had to take it. His partner was going to speak with a client the next day and the sale was important since it was for a small office building. He entered the tiny kitchenette and put the wine he had brought in the small refrigerator. He wasn't much on the stuff, but Jacqueline loved it. The cheaper the better was what she told him. He tossed beers in after it and went looking for her.

He found her curled up sound asleep on the large bed, a magazine draped across her chest. He felt a bit disappointed, but wanted her fully rested and ready for what he had planned for them. Besides, they had all weekend and he was going to make every minute count.

Chapter Five

Jack stretched and snuggled back into the warmth of the covers. The bed linens smelled softly of lavender and were smooth to the touch. She rubbed a corner between two of her fingers sleepily. She idly wondered how lavender had gotten in her sheets. Was it in her new fabric softener? Her mind wandered aimlessly, but no answer readily appeared. Slowly, she opened her eyes and looked around at the surroundings. Heavy rich burgundy curtains covered the wall she could see. A small nightstand was also in her eyeshot, and she could see a digital clock glowing softly in the murky darkness. The time read six-thirty. She closed her eyes when the day before finally came into focus. She was at the bed and breakfast with Caleb.

She opened her eyes again when she felt a solid warmth behind her. She blinked, finally realizing he was in bed with her. In fact, he was snuggled up tight behind her with their legs tangled together and one of his arms lying across her waist. She closed her eyes, understanding she must have fallen asleep the night before. She hadn't thought she was overly tired, but the stress of the week and the comfort of the bed must have acted as an instant sedative. Since he was in bed with her, she finally had the answer to what the sleeping arrangement was going to be. Unless he was in here because there was no place else to sleep. She was sure the brochure said something about a hideaway bed in the couch, but hell why should he sleep there?

He was the one who paid for the trip. If anyone slept on the couch, it would be her. But why didn't he wake her up? Maybe he had tried, but she hadn't moved.

"Babe, you're thinking way too hard for this early in the morning."

His low growl sent shivers up her spine. Fuck, he sounded sexy in the morning.

"Jacqueline, I know you're awake."

"Caleb, I know I'm awake too."

He gave a low chuckle sending warm breath right on her neck. There was no way this should make her wet, but for some bizarre reason it did. Okay, it probably had to do with his closeness and the fact she could feel him getting hard right against her backside. Without thinking, she wiggled to get better situated and froze.

"Well, baby, you've got me awake now." He nuzzled her neck lazily.

"Caleb, what is going on?" Her voice came out sounding a bit breathy and she almost rolled her eyes. What the fuck? Was she some bimbo off a porn flick?

"Lay still, baby, and let me make you feel good," he whispered softly against her neck. He moved his hand from around her waist slowly up her top. His hand was large and warm and felt right against the skin of her bare belly. He palmed her breast and began to knead and pull gently at her nipple. The breath caught in her chest as she arched to push more of her breast into his hand. His work-roughened fingers created a rasping sensation against her nipple, making it stand up taut and straight.

"You have great tits, baby. I can't wait 'til I can get my mouth around them. Would you like me to suck your tits, baby? Would you like me to lick and suck on your nipples?

Maybe bite them a little. Cause sometimes a little pain can make the pleasure a little bit better. Hmm, do you want me to?"

"Yes," she whispered, pushing her ass back into his enormous cock. She couldn't believe how turned on she was getting from him playing with a boob and whispering in her ear. Moisture pooled between her legs and she could feel it begin to slick her thighs. Restlessly she moved her legs as she tightened her thighs, gently rubbing at her own clit.

"No, Jacqueline," he told her as he pushed a leg between hers forcing the friction on her clit to stop. "I'll give you pleasure. You are not allowed to give it to yourself. Do you understand?"

She nodded as he began to push her jammy pants down. Eagerly she helped him, wanting only to have those rough fingers stroking the hot flesh between her thighs. She could feel more moisture slowly ease out of her body and dampen the lips protecting her entrance.

"Now, let's see what we have here." He bit her on the shoulder as he slid his hand between her legs. He moved his fingers gently around the outside lips of her labia, not touching her clit at all. Mindlessly, she opened her legs farther, needing him to touch her. "Fuck, baby, your pussy is wet. And it feels damn good. I can't wait till I lap up all your sweet juice. Would you like that? Would you like me to lick and suck on your pussy? Do you want me to rim your hole with my tongue? Stick it up inside of you as far as it will go?"

She nodded, unable to speak, as he slicked his fingers around her clit. Once again, he slid his leg between hers and pushed her leg up, giving him more room. He used his whole hand as he pinched her clit gently and finally plunged a finger up inside of her. Jacqueline gasped and thrust herself against his hand, beginning to ride it.

"Damn, baby, you're tight. I can't wait to get my cock inside of you. You're gonna squeeze me. But I have to get you ready. I don't want to hurt you." Saying this, he eased Jacqueline over until she was lying on top of him with her back against his front. He kicked the covers off exposing them both to darkness and cool air. He inserted his legs between hers and pushed them farther apart. He began to thrust two of his large fingers inside of her now, while the other hand toyed and pinched at her breasts. She could do nothing but writhe on top of him and hope he put her out of her misery soon. She had never felt like this before. So open, so hot, so ready.

"Fuck, Jacqueline, your pussy feels like heaven. You're sopping wet. I'm gonna eat you up like ice cream on a hot day. Get ready because I'm going to put three fingers in you. Talk to me, baby, tell me what you feel, what you like or I'll stop."

"God, Caleb, don't stop." Jack reached down and put her hand over his. She could feel the moisture from her body coating his fingers. This turned her on even more. "Your fingers are big and they fill me up."

"Not as full as you'll be when I get my dick inside of you. I'm going to pull your legs wide open, baby, and thrust so deep inside of you. You'll be mine, Jacqueline. Do you understand? You'll be mine."

She nodded, again unable to speak. As long as he kept making her feel like this, she would be his forever. He thrust his fingers inside of her faster as he ground his palm against her clit. Jacqueline shoved her hips up to his hand and began to scream as the orgasm overwhelmed her. But he wasn't finished. Caleb never stopped moving those incredibly talented fingers. Impossibly, she felt another orgasm build. She widened her legs as she ground her clit against his palm. He pushed his hand back at her, which sent her over the edge again.

"Baby, you feel so good. Your pussy clenches my fingers like it doesn't ever want to let them go. I can't wait 'til I fuck you. It's gonna be excellent."

Jack slumped back against him feeling limp and totally satiated. Even her vibrator at home didn't make her feel like this. Only Caleb had. Caleb with his large hands and whispering voice. The talking was as much a turn-on as the touching. She didn't understand why Claire hadn't liked it. Hearing him made her hotter. And he was all hers for two entire days.

Caleb lay with Jacqueline still sprawled across him. She was so hot she burned him up. He couldn't believe how responsive she was. And how hard and ready she made him by doing something simple like saying his name. He closed his eyes and knew he didn't want to just fuck her. Hell, it had never only been about the sex. He wanted all of her. He had to admit to himself, if not to anyone else, why he was glad Claire broke the engagement. He wanted Jacqueline, body and soul. He had been too fucking stupid to realize it. No, not stupid, blind. He had always gone for the blondes, petite blondes like Claire. And in doing so, he's almost lost out on perfection.

He slid Jacqueline's limp body off his own and turned her to face him. God, she was beautiful. Her eyes were sleepy with passion and her sable hair tousled and sexy. He brushed the hair out of her face and leaned forward to claim her lips. The kiss was lazy and unhurried as he eased his tongue forward to gently tease hers. She tasted of mint and heat, a flavor he would always associate with Jacqueline.

He could feel her hand drift down over his taut stomach muscles, which contracted at her gentle touch. Her hand was like a brand against his flesh, claiming the territory it drifted over. Needing her to claim him as much as he claimed her. She had promised to be his and he planned on making her keep the promise.

Jacqueline's hand skimmed lower and caressed his cock through the sweatpants he had worn to bed. God, her hand felt like heaven even through the heavy fleece. But this morning was not about his pleasure, only hers. He put a hand down and stopped her movements.

"No, Jacqueline." He nuzzled her neck and breathed in her rich fragrance. "This time was for you. Nothing else."

"Yes, Caleb," she whispered back. "I want to touch you."

"No, baby, no. I wanted this morning to be all about your pleasure."

"But touching you gives me pleasure." She slid her hand from his and plunged it down the front of his pants. She encircled his cock with her hand and rubbed up and down, forcing a moan from between his clenched teeth. "And what a big pleasure it is too. And it's all for me. My Valentine gift."

"Every bit of it," he groaned out. "Fuck, your hand feels like heaven."

"Tell me what you want," she whispered against his ear. "Am I doing it right?"

"I want you and you're doing great. Tighten your grip a bit." He reached down and tightened her hand around his cock, teaching her what gave him the most pleasure. He felt her shift and her other hand joined in the fun. He pulled his knee up until his foot was flat on the mattress, giving her more room. He opened his eyes to see a frown of concentration on her face as she gripped and pulled at his dick. The sight of Jacqueline in his bed, giving him pleasure, sent him right over before he could stop himself. His balls tightened and his orgasm rushed over him. He bucked once, twice, and came in a rush over her hands.

Caleb rested his forehead against Jacqueline's and tried to catch his breath. Any thoughts or plans he may have had slipped right out of his head as soon as she had put her hands around his dick. Damn, she was lethal. He wanted this morning to be about her pleasure and nothing else, but she had turned the tables on him. Now looking back, he didn't mind too much at all. And from the way she still held him in her hands, she didn't mind much either.

Jack snuggled next to Caleb, holding him hot and heavy in her hands. Damn, she didn't even have to look to know he was well built. She could feel it. The events of the morning had swept her along at the speed of light, giving her no time to even think. Instead, all she could do was react... And what a reaction. All he'd had to do was touch her and she was blown away. She wondered what else he had in mind. If it was anything like what had already happened, she couldn't wait.

He rubbed his lips gently over hers and skimmed them with his tongue. She guessed this answered her question once and for all why they were on this trip. He said they needed time to build their own relationship. She wondered if he had planned this or had it happened just because they happened to share the same bed.

"Baby, you're thinking hard again. You need to stop," he murmured, moving his lips down to nuzzle her neck.

"What should I be doing?" she asked, slowly gliding her hands over and around his length.

He bussed her quickly on the lips. "Getting dressed. We need to go to breakfast. I want us to explore the town, spend some time together."

“Isn’t this spending time together?” she asked, a bit confused.

“Yeah, but I didn’t bring you here to spend the whole time in bed. As much as I would love it, by the way, it still isn’t the whole reason.” He smiled and popped her on the rear. “Now go get ready because I am starving, woman.”

Jacqueline eased her hands slowly up his body. “Okay.”

“Tease,” he called after her as she hurried to the bathroom.

Jack shut the door and leaned against it. What the fuck had happened? Okay, she knew what had happened. It was obvious since she was sticky from both herself and Caleb. But he had never given her any indication this was where he even wanted the relationship to go. But it was apparent from his words this was the plan. Why hadn’t he said anything? Unless he was afraid she would have said no. Caleb afraid? The man wasn’t afraid of anything.

She shook her head. He was right—she was thinking way too hard. She needed to go with the flow and enjoy what was happening instead of analyzing every detail. She pulled toiletries out of her bag and climbed into the shower, deciding to enjoy the moment. She didn’t have to know every single thing to have a good time. The only important thing was Caleb wanted her and he made her feel like no one else had. Tucking her thoughts away, she began to wash her hair.

Chapter Six

Jacqueline walked hand in hand with Caleb around Bridge Point, the town close to the B&B. There were a variety of small shops featuring everything from handmade chocolate to wine from a local winery. What Jack did not see was a bridge or a point. She thought maybe the town might be too small to house either one. She was interested in the winery, though, since she had never seen the actual process, only read about it in a magazine. Caleb instantly had gotten directions so they could go there the next day to see how they made one of her favorite beverages.

"Yeah, but do you think they make cheap sweet wine?" She smiled at him.

"I don't know, babe, we can ask. I still don't see how you drink it."

"It's good. It's sort of like...kool-aid with a kick."

"I've never heard it described in such a way before."

"Hey, better than nasty beer. Yuck." She made a face and shivered. "The stuff looks and tastes like what I would imagine pee water would."

He laughed. "Not the good stuff."

"Is there such a thing?"

"Yes, and when we get back, I'll make sure to get some of the good stuff so you can taste it."

They wandered from shop to shop, talking and laughing, as comfortable as they had always been. If Jack didn't know it, the morning might never have happened. Except for Cal holding her hand, the hand-holding was something new. She liked the way her hand felt in his, the way he rubbed his thumb over the back of hers, as they explored the town.

They ended up having dinner at the only restaurant in town. It was early, but since they had eaten breakfast at nine-thirty, they were both starving. Jack could feel anticipation rising. She couldn't wait to get back to their cottage. She almost laughed since she had never looked forward to sex before. But she'd never been with Caleb before. He was beyond sexy. She tried not to dwell on some of the things he had said during the day. Statements making her think he wanted something beyond this brief weekend. Those thoughts led her into dangerous territory, causing the worries to resurface. Worries that made her think maybe she was someone safe for him to slip back into dating with after his broken engagement. Someone he knew and didn't have to try too vigorously with.

"You're thinking too hard again, Jacqueline."

His low voice brought her back to their meal and she smiled. "Sorry, my mind wandered."

"What has you preoccupied?" He watched her steadily.

"Nothing. Thoughts. It's not important."

"It must be something important or you wouldn't be thinking as hard as you have." When she didn't answer, he smiled. "Okay, you can keep it to yourself for now. But before we go home, you'll tell me."

"You sound very sure of yourself."

"I am." He wiggled his eyebrows at her. "I have ways of making you talk."

She burst out laughing. "Uh oh, I'm in trouble now. I guess I'd better watch out for you."

"Yep, when you least expect it, I'll spring. Just not right now." He pushed his empty plate away. "I ate too much for any leaping around."

The two of them finished dinner and Caleb paid as they headed out into the darkening night. Jack hated when it got dark before six-thirty, since it always got much colder too. She wrapped her arms around herself as they headed to the SUV. Caleb pulled her to his side to drape an arm around her waist until he could tuck her into the passenger seat. She had never been with someone who took such good care of her before. Hell, he had treated her great before, when he and Claire had been engaged. But now it was even better since they were more involved. Again, her thoughts strayed to the whys of the situation, but she quickly tossed them away. She knew Caleb; he was relentless when he wanted to know something. And this was something she wasn't ready to share. As soon as a woman tried to talk about a relationship, the man always ran for the hills. And their relationship thus far had consisted of going away for the weekend and heavy petting. Neither one, made any kind of relationship.

Caleb started the vehicle and cranked the heat to high. She loved his vehicle since the heater was actually putting out warm air before they ever made it back to the cottage. She held her hands up to the vent and sighed.

"Better?" he asked, looking over at her.

"Oh yeah, my car never gets this warm this fast."

"Is there something wrong with it? Do you need me to look at it?"

"It's an older car, Cal." She shrugged settling back in her seat. "Nothing works the way it does when you first get it."

"Have you thought about buying a new car?"

"Yeah, I think about it. Then I look at my fantastic teacher salary and know it's not gonna happen. Lisa and I joke about buying a car together and sharing, but we realized we'd have to live together too." Jack smiled thinking about her friend. "She says all we'd need is about a dozen cats. You know, to set the scene for us. She said the boys would go crazy for us."

Caleb pulled into the parking lot and Jack waited patiently for him to come around to her side of the car. It still felt odd, but good for a change, to have someone take care of her. Not since she was a child had she felt so cared for. He opened the car to help her out and they walked briskly to the cottage. Unlike last night, she distinctly heard the water on the lake tonight. She realized she had probably been asleep on her feet since that's the only way she could have missed the sound. The air was biting with the scent of moisture on the air. She hoped it was only the water she smelled and not snow heading in. As a kid, she had loved snow days, but as a teacher, she hated them since they not only threw her whole schedule off, but also extended the school year.

Once inside, Caleb helped her off with her coat and pulled off his own. Jack kicked off her shoes and settled on the couch. Jeez, she loved lazy days. If she had been home, she most probably would have spent the whole day grading. Instead, she had spent it with a sexy man. She looked up to find him watching her as he slowly took off his shoes and began to remove his watch.

"Do you want to watch TV for a while?" She looked around for the remote.

He shook his head. "No."

"Do you have something in mind you'd like to do?"

He nodded as he pulled his shirt out of his pants and began to unbutton it. "Most definitely."

"Would you like to share?" Jack smiled as he slowly revealed his broad chest to her gaze.

"First, I'm going to watch you suck on my dick. Because I can't wait to feel your mouth sucking and licking me. I'm going to strip you down after, lay you across our bed and lick your pretty pussy until you scream for me. I'll probably do it again because I know you're going to taste so sweet." He shrugged his shirt off and dropped it on the floor. "After I do all that, I'm going to spread your legs wide and feed my cock in as deep as it will go. And I'll fuck you 'til you won't be able to walk or even think about some other boys to drive crazy. What do you think?"

"Like you have everything planned out," she said. "Do I get a say in what we do?"

"No." He slowly unbuttoned his jeans. "Because this morning you said you were mine. And I want to show you what being mine is all about."

"You sound serious," Jack murmured, not believing how the more he talked the wetter she got. If anyone else had even imagined saying the things to her he did, she would have kicked his ass already. But Caleb, Caleb was different. She wanted him like she had never wanted anyone before. The L-word surfaced and she shoved it down. There was no way. Because to feel those kind of emotions would give her more pain than she wanted. Especially when the weekend was over.

"You're thinking again, baby. Remember I told you what would happen if I caught you at it again." He shoved his jeans and underwear off at the same time. Jack's breath caught in her throat. Fuck, Claire hadn't been kidding. He was hung. And her first thought was to wonder how he would taste as she took him in her mouth. If she could fit all of him in. But half the fun would be trying.

She licked her lips without thinking and he smiled slowly. "What are you thinking about?"

She shook her head. "Nothing. It's not important."

"But it is. You keep letting it pull you away from our time together." He crouched by her chair, his huge cock inches from her hand. "Tell me."

"Caleb—" she began, but he cut her off.

"Don't fucking lie to me, baby. That's not what I want between us. Tell me what's going through your mind."

Jack thought about lying, but what the fuck? What did she have to lose? After this short weekend, she doubted they would see much of each other. No matter what he said.

"What do you want between us?" she finally asked. "You invite me here for the weekend, but I had no idea for what. You said it was to build our relationship, but we didn't have this kind of relationship. Before I knew what was happening you were touching me and I loved it. Now you're sitting here naked and all I can think of is how I'm going to get your dick in my mouth and what it's going to taste like. Because I figure I might as well enjoy all this as much as possible. Because come Monday, you are going to regret all of this. You'll call me at first, but it will slowly die off. I'll see you out someplace with some cute blonde hanging on your arm and you'll ignore me. See, I already know all this. I'm already preparing for it, because if I don't it'll break my heart. And I don't want you to break my heart, because you will and you can."

Jack blinked, realizing she was crying. God, she hated tears. They were weak. She angrily wiped them away and looked back at Caleb who hadn't moved nor spoken. "So see, you probably didn't want to know what I was thinking."

Caleb stood quickly, an angry look crossing his face. He reached down and dragged her up into his arms, smashing her lips to his. The kiss was brutal in its intensity. He wrapped a hand in her hair and jerked her head back, forcing her lips open with his tongue. He thrust his tongue into her mouth as he ground his cock into her belly. All she could do was hold on as his passion overwhelmed her. She wasn't scared, far from it. She was turned on and if he let her go, she was sure she would slide right onto the floor unable to get up.

She felt them moving, but didn't realize where they were until he tossed her onto the bed. He stood before her, breathing heavily, teeth clenched. Neither one of them moved as they stared at one other. He moved toward her as Jacqueline felt finally able to draw a breath.

"Baby, I hope you're not attached to any of this clothing." He ripped her jeans open and pulled them off. He grabbed the front of her shirt and pulled it apart, sending buttons flying around the room. Quickly, he divested her of it and tossed it off into a corner. She lay stunned, still in her bra and panties. What the hell?

"It's unfortunate you chose to assume so much about this weekend," he ground out between gritted teeth. "You should have talked to me sooner. The next time I'm sure you will. But this time let me make where we stand as clear as possible. You are mine, no ifs, ands or buts. You told me you were this morning and I'm holding you to your promise. I've wanted you pretty much since I saw you, but got caught up in the stereotype I always find myself with. That's my problem, not yours. But assuming this weekend is it between us is your problem."

She opened her mouth to speak, but he held up a finger. “Don’t, baby, it’s my turn to talk.” He ripped her panties off and tossed them over his shoulder. “Like I said, you’re mine. Your pussy, your tits, all mine. I’ll kill the first man who so much as looks at you the wrong way.” He pushed her legs apart and climbed between them. “I am all yours, every single bit of me, my heart included. Do you understand, Jacqueline? This isn’t some weekend fuck, this is forever. I love you. Once we leave this place, we’ll go home, figure out where we’ll live and when we’ll get married. Because I am not letting you out of my sight again. Now if this isn’t something you want, you’d better let me know right now.”

Love! He had actually said the love word, in connection with her. Jack blinked, staring up at his magnificent body poised over her. Slowly, she sat up and thrust her breasts forward as she unhooked her bra. She tossed it off the bed and laid back down again, feeling sexy and wanton spread out before him.

“Of course, I love you. I think I’ve always loved you. I wouldn’t be here if I didn’t. I never go away with someone for the weekend. Only you.”

He blinked, a slow smile spreading across his face. “Say it again.”

“I love you.”

“Again.”

“I love you.”

“Who do you belong to?”

“You, Caleb, only you.”

“And I plan on showing you over and over.” He grabbed a pillow from the top of the bed and slid it under her bottom. He pushed his enormous shoulders between her legs and pinned her gaze with his own. "Lean up on your arms and watch me eat this pretty pussy that belongs to me."

Jack did what he asked, never taking her eyes away from his. Slowly, so slowly, he leaned forward and licked her from her anus to her clit. She gasped, but refused to look away. Instead, she tried to spread her legs farther apart to give him as much access as possible.

He smiled at her and leaned forward again to swirl his tongue around her clit. The sensations from the small movement were incredible. Jack realized now she had truly been missing out, but she wouldn't any more. Caleb obviously enjoyed this as much as she did as he put his lips and teeth to work along with his tongue. He suckled on her clit and bit it gently; unconsciously she jerked her hips up. He hummed as he rimmed the opening of her vagina with his tongue and without warning thrust it up inside of her. She couldn't help but cry out as she ground her aching slit against his hot tongue. It was heaven and hell all wrapped into one package. Never taking his mouth from her, he slid his hand up and began to twirl her clit between two big fingers.

"Come for me baby," he told her as two fingers took the place of his tongue. He thrust them deep once, and again as Jacqueline's orgasm rushed up, grabbing her, shaking her as she had never been shaken before. He withdrew his fingers covered with her essence and slowly stuck them in his mouth to suck them clean.

"I knew you'd be sweet and I'm dying for another taste." Matching his actions to his words he began to lap and suck at her pussy, pulling all the juice she produced into his mouth. He drank her as if he were dying of thirst and she the only thing to quench it. Impossibly, Jack could feel another orgasm building as she dropped her head back and screwed her eyes shut, reaching, reaching... It hit and she gasped as she could feel moisture gush out. Caleb lapped and sucked between her legs, drinking up every last bit.

Not able to hold herself up any longer she slid boneless to the bed. She pushed her sweaty hair away from her face and tried to catch her breath. But it was difficult with Caleb still eating her out. The man was insatiable and he was hers. He had said. He said marriage. He said love. More moisture gushed from between her legs as another small orgasm hit. Damn she was lucky, unless she didn't survive. But hell what a way to go.

Chapter Seven

Caleb looked up to see his Jacqueline laid out flat, a totally satisfied smile on her lips. Fuck, she tasted like fine chocolate. He couldn't get enough of her. Her pussy was ripe and so ready. He'd given women head before, but he had never loved it as much as he did with Jacqueline. Her taste, her smell –she was a delicacy waiting to be eaten up. And she was all his, forever.

"Are you okay, baby?" he asked, as he pulled the pillow out from under her.

"I think you killed me," she replied, never opening her eyes.

He crawled up her body, licking and tasting as he went. He stopped at her breasts to suckle each nipple. Her arms stole around him to cup the back of his head and hold him in place. Her tits were almost as good as her pussy. They were lush and full and made for a man to suck on them for hours.

"Do you like this?" he asked raising his head to look at her.

She opened her eyes and smiled. "I love it. I love you."

He never thought he would hear those words from Jacqueline's lips. But now he had he wanted to hear them constantly. She was everything he wanted, searched for. He had just been too damn dumb to realize it. Thank God, he had come to his senses. Because truth be told, if Claire hadn't broken the engagement, he would have. He never would have married her, he knew it now. Only Jacqueline made him feel whole, only she could satisfy him.

"I love you," he told her before claiming her lips. The kiss was lazy and slow, sexy in its unhurried exploration of each other. His tongue tangled with hers, thrusting gently as he had done into her eager slit. He could feel her hands move down his back, caressing, touching. He wanted her to know his body as well as he was beginning to know hers. He wanted her to claim him, something he had never wanted before. And with each sweep of her hands, she did claim him. No one before had ever made him want the things this woman did. Home, children, permanence.

Her hand closed around his cock and pulled gently. "Now what do I have here?" she teased. "It feels like a present for me. My Valentine's Day present."

Caleb laughed. "Spread your legs wider and I'll give you your gift."

"You told me earlier you wanted to watch me suck your dick. You wanted to see what it looked like when I took you in my mouth. And truthfully, I want to." She licked her lips. "I want to taste you like you've tasted me."

Caleb sat back quickly, her hand still wrapped tight around his cock. "Whatever the lady wants."

She let him go as he pushed the pillows up to the headboard and leaned against them. He didn't want to miss one minute of Jacqueline loving him. He spread his thighs as she crawled forward to sit between his outstretched legs. He watched her carefully as she wrapped her hand around his cock and inspected him. He knew some women were obviously put off by the size, but fuck, it wasn't like he could do something about it. Leaning forward, she swirled her hot tongue around the head and he jerked, unable to stop himself.

"Do you like when I do this?" she asked, her breath caressing his length.

"Whatever you do to me I like."

"Tell me what you want. I love it when you talk to me."

Caleb smiled, loving her all the more. "Baby, I want to watch you suck on as much as you can. I told you earlier I wanted to see my dick in your mouth. Fuck, I want to watch you suck on it like you do a Popsicle."

"Now there's an idea."

Jack sat between Caleb's legs and looked her fill. God, he was incredible, all taut muscles and sinew. And his penis was so large she could feel herself get wet imagining him thrusting inside of her. She knew it would be a tight fit and couldn't wait 'til he held her down and started feeding himself deep inside of her.

"You're thinking again, baby."

"I know. I'm thinking I can't wait for you to fuck me. I can't wait to feel how tight the fit will be for us." Jack couldn't believe the things coming out of her mouth, but with Caleb, they were right. She wanted him to know exactly how she felt.

"Damn, baby, you are making me fucking hot." He leaned forward and kissed her. "But you'll have to wait. If you're a good girl and suck Daddy's dick like you should, you'll get your reward."

She swallowed hard, feeling herself cream at his words. She never thought someone talking dirty would turn her on, but Cal did. Hell, him breathing turned her on and it only got more intense as the weekend went on. She wondered if she'd be able to get through the days next week without any sexual contact at all. She had gone from nothing to being constantly satisfied and she didn't want to go back.

"Do it, baby." He leaned back and spread his legs wide. His cock was heavily veined and hard; it pulled up toward his stomach. He wrapped a hand around the wide base and tilted it toward her. "Take my dick in your mouth. Suck on me like you do your favorite ice cream."

Jack licked her lips in anticipation. She leaned forward and placed her hands on his hips as she swirled her tongue around the large purplish head, slowly easing down the side. Clamping her lips around his dick, she sucked up and around as she did to stop her Popsicle from dripping. Opening her mouth, she slid the length into her mouth and began to gently bob her head.

Caleb dropped his head back at the sensations. "Fuck, baby, you're good at this." He kept one hand wrapped at the root so she wouldn't take too much and twined his fingers through her hair. "Come on, baby, fucking eat me. Lick me, baby, that's right, suck on it."

He tasted like hot, hard man and smelled like a decadent dessert. She experimented clamping her lips around him and sucking as she pulled up. It was hard, though, since he was so big. She had given head before, but certainly to no one built like this. And she hadn't enjoyed it. She had done it because her partner wanted her too. Now, she couldn't wait. In fact, her mouth watered at the sensation of Caleb's penetration. Carefully, she swallowed the saliva gathered in her mouth and he gasped.

"Do that again, baby, try to swallow my cock. It felt amazing." Caleb gripped her hair, the pain oddly adding to the pleasure. He guided her head in the rhythm he wanted. "Yeah, baby, suck my cock. Damn, Jacqueline, your mouth is like heaven. It's burning me up. You suck me good, baby. Do you like it? Like sucking my cock?"

She nodded, unwilling to let him slip from her lips. Because she did love the feel of him sliding over her tongue, easing over the roof of her mouth. She would love to take him all the way to the root, but knew he would never fit. Instead, she worked steadily to pull as much of him as she could into her mouth. She wanted to give him the same pleasure he gave her.

"Baby, I can't hold on much longer," Cal murmured, thrusting up to meet her mouth. "If you don't want me to come in your mouth, you'll need to pull away."

Jack sucked harder, wanting to taste him, swallow him, and take a part of his essence into her. Her jaw was beginning to tire, but she refused to let go. She wanted her reward.

"Yeah, baby, hold on. I'm gonna come, Jacqueline, and I want to watch you swallow every bit. I need you to drink me down, baby." Caleb gasped and thrust once, twice, flooding her mouth. He was hot and tasted like the sweetest wine to her as she continued to suck and swallow every last drop.

Jack pulled away from him and licked her lips, like a cat who had eaten a bowl of very good cream. He was slumped back against the pillows, face flushed, panting for breath. She crawled up his body to settle her naked flesh against his. Gently, she brushed her lips against Caleb's.

"You taste good," she whispered against his lips.

He smiled. "Do you even know how much I love you? How much I want you? I'll never get enough of you." He moved his lips down her neck and gently bit her, laving the small hurt with his tongue. "You make me whole, Jacqueline."

She wrapped her arms around him feeling tears gather. "I love you. You are the sexiest man I have ever met, the smartest and the cleverest. And you can make me have an orgasm by touching and talking to me."

"Do you like when I talk to you?"

"I love it. It makes me hot, makes me wet."

"Good, that's good." He gathered her close and rolled until she was lying under him. "Don't go anywhere. I'm going to start our fireplace. It's getting a little chilly in here."

Jack pushed the covers down the bed as Cal found the remote and pushed the button. A full fire burst into flames. She watched as the light danced over his body. He was mouthwatering. He adjusted the flame for the fire and Jack knew she could gain pleasure by looking at him. He turned back to face her and she realized he was hard again. Wow, normally men took forever to recover, but obviously not Cal.

He followed her gaze downward and smiled. "Did I mention I want you? I've thought about you for weeks, fuck, months. I've masturbated to images of you sucking my dick, to me fucking you every which way including waiting for you in the dark and grabbing you."

"Really?" She moved toward him.

"Does it turn you on?" He walked over to where she knelt on the bed. "The thought of me jacking off to images of you and me together?"

She swirled a tongue around one of his nipples. "Yes, but I get turned on when you breathe."

He laughed low as he put his arms around her. "My favorite fantasy was the one where I imagine hiding in your house. I'd watch you come home and slowly strip your clothes off. I can see you while you take a shower, the water dripping slowly down your body. As you climb out, I turn all the lights off and come up behind you. I grab you from behind and press your body to mine. I feel your pussy and it's all wet, gushing with moisture."

Caleb slid a hand over her bottom, curling it under to thrust two fingers into her vagina from behind. Jack moaned and rode his hand. His words, once again, turned her on, making her ache inside.

"I don't want you to know who I am, so I blindfold you and carry you into the bedroom. I make you lie on the bed on your stomach. I force you to go up on all fours. You are open and ready for me, even though you're scared. I lick your pussy, exactly like I did today and you push back into my face, loving it. I take you around the waist and thrust my cock into you. You're burning up inside and tight like a fist. I almost come before we get started."

"Caleb, I want you." Jack kissed him, thrusting her tongue in his mouth. This time she was acting as the aggressor. She sucked at his tongue, desperate for him to be inside of her.

"You ready for me, baby?" he asked, his voice as unsteady as her heart.

"Yes, now."

Cal came onto the bed with her and eased them both prone. He moved his hands and lips over her body until Jack was sure she would pass out. Damn, she'd be embarrassed if she did, especially before they had even gotten to the good part. He moved between her legs and she could feel him hard and hot against her belly. She curled her hips up and looped her ankles around his waist. Doing this, she could feel the large head of his cock play across her vaginal lips.

"Not yet." He took her legs from around his waist and pinned them to the bed. "Baby, are you on the pill?"

"Yes." She nodded. "For about eight years now."

"I want you to know I'm clean. I've been checked and haven't been with anyone in months."

"I had a clean bill of health at my last doctor's visit."

He kissed her. "Baby, I want to be inside of you so much. I have condoms with me, but let me in, skin against skin. I've never done it before, but I want it to be with you. I don't want anything between us. I want to be able to feel myself come inside of you."

Jack smiled and kissed him back. "I want to feel you too. Just you and me."

"Always." He balanced over her on one arm and he took his erection in hand. He teased the large head around her vaginal lips, over her clit, and finally positioned himself at her opening. "Baby, I can't wait anymore. Next time, I swear, we'll take more time."

"Hurry." She pulled her legs open wider, trying to thrust towards him. "I don't want more time. I want you now."

When she pushed up, he shoved back, lodging the head of his cock into her small opening. He began to rock slowly, moving his large member into her hot passage. Jack moved her hands over the bunched muscles of his back and down to his ass. She wanted more, now, before she died. She pulled him toward her, forcing him in deeper. She moaned when he grabbed her hands in one of his own and pinned them above her head.

"No, baby, I don't want to hurt you. You're so fucking tight. You grip me like a glove. Damn, I feel like I'm going to go off before I can even get all the way inside you." He rocked his cock deeper and deeper still. He felt like a bar of hot iron embedded inside of her sheath. He was large, almost too large, but it felt superb. Jack raised her hips, wanting more, needing more.

"Damn you, Caleb, harder. Fuck me harder," she shouted between gritted teeth. "Please."

"We'll both probably regret it." He let her arms go and gripped her hips in both of his large hands. In one motion, he thrust his tongue in her mouth and his dick all the way up inside of her. Her eyes rolled back in her head from the pleasure and pain of it. He was in so deep he was buried against the very top of her womb. She wrapped her legs around his waist and her arms around his shoulders and began to grind herself against him. He pulled out and slammed home again. She could feel his balls slap her ass and she had never felt anything as good as this before. If she died right now, she would be truly and thoroughly happy.

Caleb looped his arms around her legs and pulled them up higher to give him better leverage. He began to piston his cock in and out of her clinging wet pussy. Repeatedly, he drove his hips into hers. Jack could feel the orgasm build at her toes and wash over her. She ground herself against him and dug her fingers into his back as the pleasure overtook her. She screamed, drumming her heels on his back as he kept up the relentless rhythm. Moisture gushed out of her, bathing them both in her essence.

"Fuck, baby, fuck. Too fucking good. Too fucking tight. Damn, you're burning up. I can't hold on," Caleb yelled as his orgasm hit also. Jack could feel the scalding liquid of his cum shoot out in pulses, bathing her womb and creating small orgasms.

He collapsed on top of her, both of them breathing heavy, slicked with sweat. Jack kept her arms tight around Caleb and held him close to her heart. She closed her eyes as she felt her body go limp. Her mind was finally peaceful, knowing she had discovered absolute happiness with another human being.

Jack awoke slowly and stretched. Damn, she felt very well loved. She absently rubbed at her nose; the delicate aroma of roses surrounded her. She opened her eyes to find Caleb standing by the side of the bed watching her. A small smile played about his lips. Draped over his shoulder was one of few ties he owned. In fact, it was a tie she had given him the first Christmas they had known one another.

"Hey, beautiful." His low voice stroked her like a caress.

"Hey, yourself." She pushed herself up a bit and realized she and the bed were covered in rose petals. She picked one up and rubbed the velvety petal between her fingers, releasing its fragrance.

"Happy Valentine's Day." He moved toward her slowly and removed the tie from his shoulder.

"Happy Valentine's Day." She lay back down and watched his approach. "Are you planning on wearing the tie? Because if you are, you're underdressed for it." She eyed his naked and aroused body.

"I don't plan on wearing the tie." He eased onto the bed beside her.

"What are you going to do with it?"

"I plan on tying your hands to the headboard with it."

Jack could feel moisture ease out from between her legs. Damn, she didn't know how he did it, but he always got her instantly aroused. She figured it was the combination of his smooth voice and the dirty things he said. Whatever it was, she loved it.

"Oh," she said, for lack of anything better

Suiting action to words, he took her hands in his own and looped the tie around them. Once they were tied, he raised them above her head and attached them to the headboard as he said he would. He sat back to slowly peruse her body with his hot gaze. Jack licked her lips, loving the sense of helplessness Caleb made her feel. She knew he was the only one she would have allowed to do this to her. She would never have trusted anyone else.

He spread her legs and moved to sit between them, his cock already hard. "I love you. You are everything I want, everything I need." He picked a rose petal up and gently stroked one of her nipples with it. "You're gorgeous. I am a very lucky man."

Jack could feel her nipple harden with the brief touch he had given. "I love you, too. And I'm a very lucky woman to have a man like you love her as much as you do."

He kissed her thoroughly, deeply; she could taste the love and reveled in it. He moved down to nip gently at her jaw and she tilted her head back to give him better access. She shivered as he kissed and licked his way down her throat. Her breasts, though, were his obvious destination. He pulled a nipple into his mouth and hummed, sending little shocks through her system.

"Do you like, baby?"

"Yes."

He moved to the other breast and repeated the move. "How about this?"

"Yes."

He eased down her body, lavishing each inch of skin with attention. Jack felt as if she were melting from the heat he put off. He moved her thighs farther apart as he settled between them. She looked at him and he captured her gaze, smiling. "Don't take your eyes off of me. I want you to watch me while I love you." His words were softer than any he had spoken before. She could feel tears gather at the corner of her eyes.

He leaned in and to place a kiss at the entrance of her vagina. The feel of his lips on her wet, heated flesh was overwhelming. Her breath caught in her throat as she could feel his tongue lap gently between her lips, barely catching her clit. She jerked and tried to push herself at him, wanting to hurry him along. But Caleb moved his hands to pin her down.

"You know what, baby?" Without waiting for a response, he plunged his tongue up into her vaginal opening.

As an answer, all she could do was gasp and try to grind her pussy into his mouth. His hands held her tight though, not allowing her to move. She spread her legs farther apart, feeling an orgasm beginning to build. Not even her trusty vibrator could bring her off this fast.

He removed his tongue and smiled at her. "I think we'll spend every Valentine's Day this way." He slid two fingers inside of her wet sheath and began sucking on her clit.

Jack gasped and moaned, agreeing with him wholeheartedly.

Epilogue

One Year Later

Caleb and Jacqueline Sinclair walked hand in hand through the front door of Willow Creek Bed & Breakfast. Their wedding had been six months earlier and they had taken a wonderful honeymoon to a secluded resort in Mexico. At least Jack thought they had gone to Mexico. Caleb had let her out of their suite so infrequently they could have stayed home for as much as she actually saw. Though she certainly wasn't complaining. She wouldn't trade their time together for all the margaritas in Mexico.

Amanda Hayden once again stood behind the desk, waiting for them with a smile. "Welcome, welcome back." She laughed as she pulled the key to the cottage out. "My goodness, young man, you must be anxious. I've never had anyone reserve the cottage a year in advance."

Caleb returned her smiled. "I promised my wife we'd come here for Valentine's Day again. I didn't want to disappoint her."

Amanda eyed him and glanced at Jack. "I doubt very much if you disappoint her in any way. I've seen plenty of couples come through here, but I remembered you two right off. You look right together, like you belong. Not many couples do." She busied about getting Caleb to sign the register.

Jack looked down at her platinum wedding band and sapphire engagement ring and smiled. Ms. Hayden was absolutely correct, he never disappointed her, and she worked hard in return to ensure he was happy and loved. She glanced up to catch him watching. His gaze was hot with promise and she knew his cock was already hard. Since she had teased and touched him the whole drive, she made sure of it.

He thanked Ms. Hayden and they exited the house by the cottage entrance. He led her quickly through the cooling air and through the green gate.

"Not anxious are you?" she teased.

He opened the door and tossed the suitcases on the floor. He turned, and swept her up in his arms. Caleb kicked the door shut and carried her to the bedroom while Jack laughed. Damn, she loved this man more with every passing day. The past year had been a whirlwind of wedding plans, house shopping and work. She still taught with Lisa at the same school, and Cal's business had gotten even busier. But no matter what, they always made time for each other. Once the day ended, they shut the door on the outside world and loved one another.

He tossed her lightly on the bed and removed his coat. Jack quickly pulled off her shoes and clothing. She was wearing her favorite sweater and didn't want to have to work to replace it. Once thing, Caleb was very hard on her wardrobe. More than once she had to toss a shirt out due to missing buttons or ripped seams. But damn, what a way for them to go.

She lay back on the bed naked and watched him slowly disrobe. He unknotted the new tie she had gotten him and draped it across the headboard. "Wouldn't want to lose it, baby. We'll be putting it to use."

Jack shivered at the sexy growl in his voice. Hot damn, she couldn't wait.

About the Author

To learn more about Gwendolyn Cease, please visit www.gwendolyncease.com. Send an email to Gwendolyn at gwendolyn_cease@yahoo.com or join her Yahoo! group to join in the fun with other readers! http://groups.yahoo.com/group/questforromance

Forever Valentine

Bianca D'Arc

Dedication

To my Mom and Dad. The two most amazing people in the universe. Followed closely by Maya and Gwen, who are sweet to share this anthology with me. Thank you ladies for a wonderful experience all around. Let me not forget our fantastic editor, Jess, without whom this anthology would not be possible.

And to my Australian friends, Megan and Rosemary. Thanks for all your helpful advice and kind support to a newbie. You're both incredibly special ladies.

Let me not forget my fantastic editor, Jess, and the wonderfully supportive people on my chat group. I couldn't do any of this without you! St. Valentine's Day has always been a kind of strange day for me filled with hopes and let-downs alike. I hope this story brings you all a little joy and an escape from the everyday, if just for a little while. Hopefully that will be my gift to you this year. Happy Valentine's Day!

Chapter One

Jena noted the vampire's presence in the little bistro almost immediately. It was hard to miss a man as handsome as Ian Sinclair. They'd met at her friend Christy's wedding. He was an old friend of the groom...a *very* old friend, considering the groom was a vampire with over two centuries under his belt.

Jena had learned about the existence of vampires the night Sebastian, Christy's new husband, saved her friend's life by turning her. Christy had been under Jena's care in the hospital, and they needed her complicity in order to save Christy's life. Christy's first husband, Jeff, had finally beat her to death, but Sebastian and his magic blood saved her and not long thereafter, Christy was free of Jeff for good and happily married to Sebastian.

As a doctor, Jena was fascinated by the idea of vampirism, though all of the vampires she now knew refused to let her get close enough to try to figure out what made their blood so different. As a woman, Jena was intrigued by the vampire's erotic power. Jena hadn't let Sebastian turn Christy without first receiving some assurance that his bite wouldn't hurt her more. No, Jena had demanded to be bitten first, so she'd know for herself Christy wouldn't suffer.

What she'd felt when Sebastian first licked her neck, then bit down and sucked hard, had been unbelievable. An intense orgasm had shuddered through her body, though she still had all her clothes on. Worse, she and Sebastian were in a hospital room full of friends, ancient and newly turned alike, who watched every spasm of her ecstasy with varying degrees of envy and amusement. Jena could have died of embarrassment, if she hadn't felt so damn good. Just the bite of the vampire, paired with his ability to influence her mind and sexual responses, had her coming for him shamelessly. And she'd only just met the man!

Jena had since learned that vampires fed not only on blood, but also on the psi energy that was strongest at the point of orgasm. Sex was sustenance to them, just as much as blood. They were erotic creatures in every sense of the word and the males who were now mated to her closest friends were sexy in the extreme. They all seemed to exude some kind of animal magnetism that was incredibly hard to resist. It helped to remember that they were married to her best friends and said friends now had sharp teeth of their own.

Then there was Ian.

A single, devastatingly handsome vampire with sad eyes that smoldered. Jena had spotted him across the reception hall at Christy's lavish wedding and from that moment on, no other man seemed to exist in her world. He was tall, handsome as sin, and just looking at him made her body cream with anticipation. Oh, he had the same sexual pull as the others, but like them, he'd never focused it on her. If he had, she was very much afraid she'd throw herself at him, strip naked in front of all the wedding guests and yank him down onto one of the catering tables to be roundly ravished.

He was just that sexy.

Sebastian had given her the best orgasm of her life—which she knew was pretty pathetic, considering they hadn't even had sex. And he'd been rushed at the time, worrying over Christy, and a little ticked off at Jena standing in his way. He'd taken her blood quickly, with little finesse, but oh, how fantastic he'd made her feel.

If Sebastian was that good on the run, she wondered what Ian could do if he took his time.

Ian Sinclair was every bit as alluring as Sebastian, and far older. What little she knew about his past came secondhand from Christy, and she'd be damned if she could understand why the man fascinated her so much. Christy told her little tidbits, such as how Ian had once been a knight. Those incredible muscles had been first built by wielding a sword, and he kept a stable of horses at one of his homes on the coast. He lived nearby, but Christy either didn't know where or wasn't telling. Jena had also heard he was employed as some kind of enforcer for the vampire organization that her other friend Kelly's new husband Marc headed.

Simply put, Ian was assigned to watch her. Watching and waiting, ready to end her life should she make any move to reveal the existence of vampires or disseminate her knowledge of their kind. He was like police, judge and executioner for his kind, keeping sacred the most important of their laws, that of secrecy. She had no doubt the man was a cold blooded killer, though the thought of him didn't send shivers of fear down her spine. Nor revulsion. No, if she shivered it was in a very sexual kind of anticipation.

Since Christy's wedding, she hadn't been able to get the man out of her mind. They had shared a dance and conversation that wasn't quite as light or banal as it should have been between strangers.

They'd started out quite normally, talking about the bride and groom. It was Ian who turned the conversation to a more philosophical discussion about the miraculous existence of love in the world, even for a couple as unlikely as Christy and Sebastian. A battered woman and an English nobleman turned vampire over two centuries before.

Ian's firm belief that there was someone for everyone touched her heart, as had the warmth in his dark eyes. After that one dance, she'd felt the heat of his gaze on her as the party progressed, and she found herself watching him as well. Not only was he a fine figure of a man, but his manners were impeccable, and he seemed to have genuine affection for his friends. When it came time to toast the bride and groom, Jena was touched by Ian's eloquent, romantic, and tender salute to the new couple.

He wormed his way into her soft heart that night, and she hadn't been able to oust him since. Of course, it was nearly impossible to forget the man, since he was watching her every time she turned around. She'd seen him observing her come and go from her small, suburban home almost every night.

Yes, every night when she came home from work he was there, watching her, making his presence known but never speaking. His quiet appearances were probably meant to be menacing, but she found his surveillance oddly comforting. In fact, when she hadn't seen him tonight, for a moment—just a moment—she'd panicked.

But it was Saint Valentine's Day and she had a date. Jena had put Ian's absence from her mind with some difficulty and prepared for her evening out.

She didn't date much these days, spending most of time at the hospital, but she didn't want to be alone on this special night. So she'd given in and finally said yes to one of her fellow doctors, Dick Schmidt, a cardiac specialist with a big ego and very expensive car to match. Normally Jena wouldn't have given such a frivolous man the time of day, but Dick had been asking her out for weeks now, and his persistence had worn her down. Plus, what single woman really wanted to be alone on Valentine's Day?

She'd agreed to dinner and a few hours later, there she was, sitting in a trendy little bistro with a man she really didn't like sitting across from her. And a drop dead gorgeous vampire eyeing her from across the room.

They sat on the enclosed patio with tinkling white lights and soft moonlight filtering in through the glass roof. It was chilly outside, but within the heated glass enclosure they had the illusion of sitting outside without the cold February air intruding.

She tried to focus on Dick's inane conversation but it was hard. For one thing, he kept trying to touch her. The man was like an octopus, though mostly respectful of the fact that they were in public. Still, he was forever reaching across the table and touching her arms, her hands, and anything else he could reach. It was repulsive.

And then there was Ian. Sitting there, his eyes hot as sin. Watching her.

It was comforting in a way, but at the same time, rather annoying. As a vampire, Ian was totally off limits, unless she wanted to be a blood donor. But she wanted more than that from a man. She wanted a home and family, a man to care for who would care for her in return. She was getting to the critical age where she needed to think of those things before she succumbed—like her ancestors before her—to the rare condition that caused her no end of worry about her future.

So she tried to ignore Ian and concentrate on getting to know Dick Schmidt better. Perhaps he really was a nice guy under all the outward flash. He deserved a chance, and heck, he was the only guy who'd asked her out in months now, so beggars couldn't be choosers. Jena tried to smile at his jokes and put all thoughts of the vampire across the small, dimly lit room out of her mind.

Of course it didn't help that Ian had a direct view of their table. The way his flashing eyes followed her every move was somewhat unnerving, but when he raised his glass of deep red wine in silent toast to her, Jena found she couldn't control the rush of blood to her cheeks. She tried to hide behind her water glass, but she knew the vampire's keen vision had picked up her blush, even in the dim lighting of the restaurant.

Ian didn't know why he was torturing himself this way. He'd watched the woman for months, and she showed no signs of betraying her friends or their secret. Her obvious loyalty counted for much in his mind. From what he had observed, the female doctor had formed deep friendships with Christy, Kelly and Lissa, the three new vampire mates who had been recently claimed and turned. The women had become fast friends in college and those bonds would not be easily broken. Jena seemed okay with the notion that some of her best friends had been converted by their new mates.

She was curious, of course, since she was a highly trained medical professional, but accepting that her friends and their new husbands were immortal. Ian admired the woman. She was strong, like the women of his clan had been back in the days of endless war with the English and then later in his travels through the Holy Land and along the Silk Road. But Jena was also soft and caring, with a gentle heart. He'd observed her at the hospital when she was on the night shift—though he was careful to mask his presence in such a public place—and he'd seen both her skill and her compassion.

He'd also watched the pathetic excuse for a man who now sat across from her ask her out on this ludicrous date. Silently, he'd been hoping she'd tell the weasel to take a hike, but to his consternation, she'd agreed to dinner with the other doctor. It had been all Ian could do not to reveal his presence and pound the smaller man into the floor for even daring to think he had a chance with this special woman.

Coming here tonight was immature, he knew, but Ian couldn't help himself. He had to watch over her. He told himself he was just doing the duty he'd sworn to perform as an enforcer for his kind, but really, he was here for himself. Jena wasn't going to tell weasel-boy about vampires, and even if she did, the mental munchkin sitting across from her wouldn't believe it. He just didn't have the imagination.

But he did have audacity. In vast quantities. Ian saw him reach across the table to snag her hand at the same time his leg moved and his sock-covered foot brushed over her calf. Jena jumped, moving her chair back so she was mostly out of reach of his marauding footsie, but she couldn't pull her hand away without causing a scene.

If that little twerp touches her one more time, Ian thought loudly in their direction, *it'll be the Saint Valentine's Day Massacre all over again.*

Really, Ian. The feminine flavored thoughts landed gently in his mind, shocking him down to his Italian leather loafers. *Please try to behave yourself.*

You heard me? It didn't seem possible the little human doctor could have any psi ability—and certainly not this kind of strong, delicious-tasting telepathy. Ian could count on one hand the number of humans he'd met over the centuries who could communicate with him this way.

Obviously. Her tone was dryly amused.

Fascinating. The observation escaped through his astonishment. *Do you make a habit of listening to other people's thoughts?*

Actually, no. I've only ever been able to pick up on really strong personalities and practically no one ever hears me when I talk back in their minds.

'Practically' no one?

Well, my mother can. And a few others.

More and more intriguing.

Dick Schmidt interrupted their silent conversation by squeezing her hand.

What do you see in a guy like that? He's on the make, plain and simple. And if you dare take Romeo home with you tonight, I may not be able to control myself.

His name is Dick.

How appropriate.

You wouldn't really hurt him, would you?

Ian paused. *I'd try not to, but honestly, Jena? I can't be certain. I don't like seeing you with him.*

But is it so wrong to want someone in my life, Ian? Compared to you, my life is so short. I want to find love, if I can. Her tone was so wistful, it lit the dark recesses where he'd buried his heart.

You won't find love with the likes of him. And you still have many years to consider, and find the man who will treat you right.

Not as many as you might think—or that I might wish for.

Ian would have asked what she meant by that cryptic comment, but Dick reclaimed her attention, shoving a small box across the table. Ian's hackles rose.

"For you, dollface." Ian's sharp hearing picked up the other man's smarmy tone.

Ian's only consolation was that Jena didn't seem all that thrilled at the prospect of receiving a gift from the other doctor. She opened the small package as if it were contagious, an expression of guarded curiosity on her beautiful face.

When she lifted the lid and dropped the box back on the table, Ian almost rose and rushed to her side, but she was quick to recover her composure. She pasted a patently false smile on her face and thanked the man for the lovely thought, but demurred from accepting what Ian now saw was a chunky silver bracelet. Even from across the room, he could smell the metallic tang of fine silver, more pure than sterling.

Poison.

Pure silver was the fastest, most painful way to kill a vampire. It reacted with the special agent in their blood and tissues, frying them from the inside out. Ian had seen one or two of his kind die that way in his many centuries and the agony of their deaths haunted him sill.

Give it back to him. I don't want that poison anywhere near you. Ian knew he was being unreasonable. She was human after all, silver wasn't lethal to her. But all his protective instincts rose when he saw the otherwise pretty ornament.

Believe me, neither do I. Silver and I just don't mix.

Jena slid the box back over to Dick using just the tip of one finger. She thanked him again for the sentiment, but explained her allergy to silver. She also said—much to Ian's satisfaction—she couldn't accept such a costly gift from a man she hardly knew.

You're allergic to silver? The idea made Ian pause. Few humans were truly allergic to the precious substance.

My skin turns black and a sort of disgusting shade of green. It's pretty gross, so I steer clear.

Curiouser and curiouser, Ian thought carefully to himself. The fair skin, the allergy to silver, preference for working the night shift...all these things suddenly made him suspicious. They brought to mind legends about how once in a very long while, a child might be born of a vampire and a mortal. It wasn't common at all, but every few hundred years or so, such things did occur.

The resulting children were often sickly, but usually survived into their thirties, and sometimes had children of their own. Demi-vampir, these oddities lived on the fringes of both worlds, often totally unaware of their connections to the supernatural unless they came into contact with a true vampire who was willing to clue them in.

Perhaps Jena, or one of her ancestors more likely, was the product of such a union? Then her abilities and proclivities would make a lot more sense. Ian wondered if she could be one of these—the rarest of the rare.

Chapter Two

Ian sat through the rest of the interminable dinner date, calmly sipping his wine, presenting a tranquil façade to the world while he inwardly seethed. Dick was really getting on his nerves. The unctuous doctor had more moves than an acrobat, and he tried every last one on Jena. But she was just a little too savvy. She verbally skirted around his glaring innuendo, and avoided his roving footsie with aplomb. Ian silently cheered her on from his ringside seat.

When it came time to leave, he was right behind them. Oh, most people wouldn't be aware he followed, but another supernatural being might just ferret him out—if they were really good.

Ian watched from the bushes at the foot of Jena's driveway as Doctor Octopus tried to charm his way inside her home. The little bastard would step through that door over Ian's dead body, and no other way. But he'd give Jena a chance to get rid of him in a more reasonable way first.

Ian didn't quite understand his own violent responses, but he knew he was far from rational where Jena was concerned. Still, he would try to play by the rules, as long as Doctor Dick didn't do anything to push Ian over the edge. He wanted so badly to pound the other man's face into the ground, he knew he had to steer clear if at all possible. Contact between himself and the smaller mortal male could very well be deadly for Doctor Dickhead.

Ian amused himself thinking up insulting variations of Dick's name while he waited impatiently for Jena to finally send the jerk on his way. Hey, it was better than ripping the man's face off. And far less troublesome.

But what had the world come to when a fearsome, centuries-old vampire had to play schoolyard games in his mind to keep from brutally biting a man he didn't like at all? Ian shook his head. It was because of Jena. Had to be. The woman was driving him crazy. It was as plain and simple as that. Before Jena had come into his life, he had been a mentally balanced, somewhat austere man. Since babysitting for the beautiful doctor, he'd become a salivating, slandering, just downright silly parody of himself.

Ian grinned in triumph when the sniveling facsimile of a man finally turned away from Jena's door in defeat. A silent pounding of his fist in the air was Ian's victory dance. He watched Dick Schmidt back his pompous luxury car out of the driveway, and followed his progress down the dark street until he was out of sight.

Only then did Ian make his way up to Jena's door. It was partially open as he knocked, and Jena stood on the other side as if expecting him. Perhaps she was, he thought with an inward quake. Perhaps she was one of the precious few mortals who could detect his kind, even when he wished to remain hidden. Or perhaps—and this was even more frightening—she was the one woman in all the world, and all the centuries, who was destined just for him.

"Will you invite me in?" Ian's voice was pitched low, his tone somber.

Jena knew the vampire had to be formally invited inside her dwelling. It was tradition, and these creatures thrived on tradition, if nothing else. But the question remained in her mind—should she? Should she invite the vampire into her home, breaching the sanctity of her only retreat?

Could she trust Ian not to take advantage? Could she trust him not to kill her, if for some reason he took it into his mind that she was a threat to his people? That was the crux of the matter right there.

Jena considered for a long moment before stepping back to make room for him to enter.

"Please come in, Ian."

"You say that with such resignation. As if you've been expecting me."

Jena shrugged. "I knew from the moment I saw you in that restaurant, you would show up here sooner or later."

Ian sighed dramatically. "How the mighty have fallen. I've become predictable in my old age."

Jena chuckled as he swept past her into the small foyer of her house. He had a quirky sense of humor and it took her by surprise.

"I'll grant that you're probably much older than me, but you give the appearance of being only a few years my senior. So the 'old age' thing just won't work."

"Ah, the impertinence of youth." His eyes sparkled with mischief. "But then what's an immortal to do?"

Jena ushered him into the small, heated greenhouse that was attached onto the back of her home. It was a refuge in the sheltering greenery of her private backyard. She kept a small wine cooler in the room for when she needed to unwind after a long day—or night—at the hospital. There were also a multitude of candles just waiting to be lit around a small patio set with a table and two chairs.

"Will you join me in a glass of Beaujolais Nouveau? Can your kind drink that?"

Ian actually shivered. "It is a delicacy to me. The first wine…the closest thing to sunshine I will ever feel again."

Jena was touched by his unexpectedly poetic words as she bent to retrieve a fresh bottle from her private stock in the wine cooler. When she straightened from her task, Ian was already seated, and several of the nearest candles were lit.

"You move fast," she nodded toward the flickering tapers.

"When the need arises." Ian bowed his head slightly in acknowledgement.

Smiling, Jena set the wine bottle before him, along with a cork screw. "Will you do the honors?"

"Gladly."

Ian made short work of the wrapper and cork, allowing the wine to breathe a bit while Jena reached behind her for a pair of crystal glasses. He really had impeccable manners, like something right out of the pages of history. But then, that's essentially what he was. He had lived in gentler times and had the manners to prove it.

Jena could not let herself forget that regardless how polite he was now, Ian was a cold-blooded killer. Not only had he embraced the darker side of existence when he became a vampire, but the work he did as an enforcer for the vampire hierarchy only honed his deadly skills. It was his job to hunt down rogues among his kind, dispense justice, and protect the secrecy of their existence from all mortals.

She guessed he had also dealt with other kinds of supernatural beings throughout his many years on earth. Intrigued, she tried to imagine just a little bit of what he had lived through in his centuries. The things he must have seen. The places he must have lived. It boggled the mind.

"I wish you wouldn't look at me like that." Ian's voice floated from out of the night. The candles were for her benefit, she knew. Vampires could see quite well in the dark.

"Like what?" She tried to be nonchalant, but it was clear she'd been caught staring.

Ian poured the wine calmly. "Like you're wondering just what horrible things I've done over the centuries."

Damn. "So are you a mind reader as well as a vampire?" Jena lifted the glass and tried to brazen it out.

"Sometimes. Though it's more my skill at reading facial expressions and body language than anything psychic. And you're wonderfully easy to read, Jena." He toasted her with his glass.

"So much for a woman's air of mystery."

Ian drank a small sip from his glass and appeared to truly savor it. The look on his face was that of a man who had touched the sublime. Jena knew the Beaujolais was good. It came from Atticus' vineyard, after all. Atticus was a vampire who had spent centuries perfecting his vines and his wine making craft.

"Oh, your mystique is in tact, doctor. Never fear." Ian cradled the glass as if it held the most precious thing in the universe. And for him, perhaps it did.

Jena's newly changed friends had told her just a bit about the vampire's relationship to wine and how alcohol somehow reacted with their body chemistry to heal them. It was about the only thing they could ingest without becoming ill and it held an almost mystical significance to them. It was their one last link to the sun.

Her friends wouldn't tell her much more, but just knowing of the existence of vampires in the world fascinated Jena. It amazed her to think her newly-turned friends would live on long after she was dead. They would remember her and perhaps in that way, she'd leave just a little of herself behind.

Depressing thoughts bothered her more and more often these days. Part of it was seeing her friends' happiness and wondering how she might find just a small portion of the same before her short time on earth was up.

They sat quietly for a while in companionable silence while the night wore on. Jena thought of the miserable date she'd just ended and the rotten luck she had with men and with Valentine's Day in particular. She'd never had a successful date on a Valentine's Day and thought the holiday was vastly overrated. Jena sighed as she sipped her wine.

"This whole Valentine's thing is for suckers."

Ian chuckled as he poured more wine for them both.

"I knew a man once who guarded Valentine in Rome, a thousand years before I was born. Valentine was a humble priest when the emperor outlawed marriage among his young soldiers. Seems he thought single men made better soldiers with no one at home to worry about. Valentine was imprisoned and killed for the crime of marrying off youngsters who had every reason in the world not to marry. Romantic fool that he was, he claimed the only true reason to wed was love."

"You're talking about Saint Valentine?" Again Jena was fascinated by the idea that this man had walked the earth for centuries and had known others who were even more ancient.

Ian nodded. "Legend has it he wrote the first Valentine note to the daughter of his jailer, a blind girl who befriended him.

When she opened his note, God granted her a miracle and she could suddenly see. He'd signed the note simply, 'Your Valentine'."

"That's such a beautiful story."

"My friend often said Valentine would have been tickled to see what's become of his name and his legend. He was a pious man for all that he enjoyed seeing young love in bloom."

"When did he live?"

Ian shrugged. "Oh, somewhere around 270 A.D., I think."

Jena was stunned by the idea. "Just how old are you, Ian?" Her whispered words reached out through the darkness.

Ian dreaded the question. At no time since his conversion had he felt the weight of his years more acutely than when sitting across from this young, vital woman. But yet, something inside him longed to be open with her, when he hadn't talked of his past with anyone in decades...perhaps centuries.

"Not quite that old, Jena. I was born in 1232, or thereabouts. Back then, the common folk didn't keep such rigorous track of the years as we do now." He waited, but Jena was silent, which surprised him. She didn't ask questions about his life, she merely waited, as if prepared to accept whatever he chose to share. Somehow that made it easier. "The Crusades were mostly over by then, but I only realize that now, by virtue of being able to look back at what seemed so important to me at the time, through the lens of history. Even though I knew it was foolhardy, I trained as a knight and followed King Louis—the ninth one—to lay siege to Tunis. Got sick as a dog from some gut rot that was going around." Ian sipped at his wine, remembering. "Louis actually died from it. To this day, I still think it was sabotage, but we couldn't prove anything."

"So you were still...human then."

Ian's eyes challenged her. "Mortal, you mean? Oh, yes, very much so. I didn't run into Dom until a year or two later. 1271 was the year I followed Marco Polo and his father to China."

"You're kidding."

Ian chuckled. Somehow it felt right to be telling her these things that he hadn't thought of in decades. "Afraid not. I was part of their traveling party. After the failed siege at Tunis, I went to Rome to seek the wisdom of a priest I'd met in my travels who lived there in service to the Pope. He knew the Polos and suggested to them that I might be handy to have along as added protection, I guess. Father Augustus counseled me to meditate on the long journey. He told me I would find my answer in the East. Or that's what he claimed God had told him. He was a funny old man that way, but back in those days I was inclined to believe when a holy man told me God spoke to him on a regular basis." Ian shrugged. "Regardless, off I went on the Silk Road to China. And there I met Domitian, the vampire who gave me the blessing and curse of immortality."

"But why?"

Ian sighed heavily. "Who's to say? Perhaps he was lonely. Dom had traveled the earth since before the time of Christ. He's the one who knew Valentine. He once told me he'd been a Praetorian Guard during the reign of at least three Caesars. We had Rome in common, though the Rome I knew was much different from the city in which he'd been born."

Ian put his half-full glass on the table, his gaze meeting hers. "As to why he changed me? Treachery. Pure and simple. There were factions that didn't want the Polos to succeed in their business venture, both rivals from their own land and isolationists and political maneuverers in the lands through which we traveled. Some were more violent than others and as a knight, it was my job to organize a defense and repulse any attacks. It's what got me killed—or as close as I've come in my long life.

"I'd already become friends with Dom. We met him on the Road and he invited us to stay at his compound while we rested for the next leg of the journey. We'd been staying with him for a few days when the attack came—raiders from the East trying to stop us before we could make it through to the Khan—but we repulsed them. I was gravely wounded in the fighting, though, and taken within Dom's private home to be treated, but I was too far gone. When Dom saw me, he decided to save me in his own way and made me what I am."

"He gave you his blood." Her tone was solemn, her eyes filled with compassion that was almost his undoing. Ian couldn't believe he'd told her so much of the past he usually kept well buried. He sighed and picked up the glass once more, twirling it by the stem between his agitated fingers.

"Forgive me. I didn't mean to dwell on things better left forgotten."

"What happened to Dom?" Her soft voice tempted him.

"I don't know, actually. He taught me all I needed to know about my new life. When the Polos continued on their way, I stayed with Dom in his compound. I stayed there for quite a while, in fact, until Dom decided to pick up stakes and move on. When he left, I did too, though traveling was a lot tougher in those days for our kind."

"I bet." Jena chuckled just slightly as she sipped at her wine. "I'm glad he saved you, Ian." Her tender tone nearly stopped his heart.

Ian paused, considering his words before speaking. "There are times I wished he'd let me die over the years, but just now, being here with you, it all seems worthwhile."

Jena blushed, her vital young blood heating her cheeks and making him salivate in anticipation. "I bet you say that to all the girls."

"I say that only to you, Jena, because it's true." He reached across the small table to grasp her hand, stilling her nervous movements.

Chapter Three

Jena thought absently how different this little tête-à-tête with Ian was when compared to the disastrous date she'd had earlier that night with Dick. For one thing, when Ian grasped her hand, her womb clenched in anticipation and excitement instead of dread. Ian was a man well out of her league and much too dangerous to her heart. How could she even entertain the idea of flirting with him when there was no way she could survive any closer encounter with him without badly bruising—if not breaking—her fragile, mortal heart?

She knew it was highly unlikely Ian would magically discover she was the one woman in all the world meant just for him. Sure, just that had happened to a few of her best friends, but what were the odds of Jena being yet another match for one of these amazing vampire studs? Not likely. Not likely at all.

Still, just looking into Ian's eyes was a pleasure she would remember all her life. When he left, she would pull out the memory of this night and warm herself with the echoes of the fire she saw in his burning gaze. His hand tightened on hers and her nerves erupted. He was getting too close. It was time to pull back in the name of self-preservation.

"Don't think you're going to sweet talk your way into a blood donation, Ian. I've been bitten once, and that was enough."

Ian sat back, breaking the contact and pulling his hand away from hers. She missed his touch immediately. His gaze was still hot though, burning over her skin as he considered her.

"Sebastian told me about it, you know."

Oh, God. Jena took a sip of her wine, hoping to cool the flush of embarrassment she knew must be staining her cheeks.

"You mean you guys bite and tell? Have you no shame?" She hoped he would go with the humor and drop the subject, but somehow she suspected he wouldn't let her off that easy.

"Sebastian drank from you in front of witnesses, and he was half out of his mind with worry, knowing he had to change Christy quickly in order to save her life, but he made a point to tell me he thought there was something odd about your blood."

"Odd? I don't think I like the sound of that."

"Special then," he conceded. "He said your essence gave him more energy than it should have, though he couldn't be sure with all the turmoil of the moment. Still, when things had settled down, he remembered it and thought it significant enough to call and tell me. He thought I should know when I was assigned to watch you."

"So why are you telling me this? Is this some elaborate way of asking for a taste? If so, I'm not buying it. I refuse to give another vampire cheap thrills and a meal."

Jena blushed furiously as she remembered the way Sebastian had fed from her, his astounding mental powers taking over her body and giving her an orgasm unequalled in her experience. In public! In front of her friends. And with all their clothes still on and his hands around her, but only to hold her upright, not in any place the least bit provocative. The man was dangerous.

And she'd bet Ian was downright lethal.

"First of all, you could never be cheap, Jena, and you'd get as much—if not more—out of it as I would." His gaze burned a path over her pebbled nipples as if he knew just how much his sexy, low voice turned her on. And he probably did too, the rat.

"Second, I really am curious enough to ask. Sebastian is relatively young compared to me and I truly wonder if what he sensed was accurate or just a product of the tense situation you were all in at the time. Third, I've observed you for the past weeks and have some theories of my own I'd like to test. Tasting your blood would go a long way toward helping me secure your future safety."

She would have questioned him on that point, but he just kept talking in his commanding way, not letting her get a word in edgewise.

"And lastly," his voice dropped even lower, sexier, "you know as well as I do that I could seduce you into baring your neck—and anything else I asked for. But I'm man enough to give you the choice. I don't want it if you don't want to give it. I'm old fashioned like that." He shrugged and tossed off the last of his wine, replacing the glass on the small table.

Holy crap.

The man was walking, talking sex on a stick. And he was thirsting for her. Or her blood, at least. With it, if he was anything like his friend, he would give her intense sexual satisfaction, but somehow she didn't think Ian would be satisfied with just giving her a mental orgasm. No, Ian would want more. He'd want skin on skin, body on body, all out, messy sex.

And she was practically salivating at the thought of it. Her womb clenched and her panties grew embarrassingly damp.

"So you want to bite me?" She had to get control of this conversation back somehow.

"In a word? Yes." Ian's eyes bored into hers. "And I want to fuck you."

Jena twirled her nearly empty glass, trying to buy time while her thoughts were in turmoil. She fought down the gulp of panic that wanted to sound from her suddenly parched throat.

"You know, that's not very romantic."

Ian stood and swept her up into his arms. She thumped into him, out of breath from his amazingly fast and forceful action. His arms came around her waist as she looked helplessly up into his exotic, mysterious eyes.

"I can be romantic." He tucked one of her hands up around his neck, taking the other lightly in his as he began shuffling her around the dim room in a slow dance.

"Ian, there's no music." How had she ended up next to his hard body, nestled so close against his muscular chest and rippling abs? He was like a drug, lulling her into compliance.

"I can fix that." Ian pointed one finger at her small stereo, switching it on with his mind and turning the dial to a slow jazz station. In seconds, soft, sexy sounds emanated from the small stereo unit and he took up the rhythm with his feet once more.

"Telekinesis too?" she asked, a bit in awe of this amazing man who held her so close to his perfect body.

Ian shrugged and she felt the slide of his solid muscles over bone under her hands. He was like Michelangelo's David, he was so hard, yet so beautifully formed.

"Over the years, my powers have increased. The telepathy and telekinetic abilities are something that grow over time along with the other psi abilities."

"You guys are amazing."

"Not quite so amazing as you, *cara*. Have you always been telepathic?" He steered her around the small room expertly to the low, erotic tones of the jazz music, his body in perfect alignment with hers. She felt his every word deep in her veins, pulsing through her body.

"My mother could always pick up on my thoughts, even as a baby, she said. Some of my earliest memories are of her speaking to me in my mind." She remembered those times in her youth fondly as Ian held her close. Something about his hold was so protective while at the same time, provocative.

"And your father?"

Jena shook her head. "He didn't have the ability and he didn't quite believe my mother and I did either, no matter how many times we did something unexplainable in front of him. He was a hard case."

"He's gone then?"

The soft ache she'd had since her father died ceased to hurt quite as much while Ian held her safe in his strong arms. "He died in a car wreck about ten years ago. It's why I decided to go into medicine."

"And your blood anomalies had no influence on your choice?"

She stopped dancing to pull back and look up at him. "How did you know about that? Did you guys have me investigated? How did you get my medical records? I thought those were sealed!"

"Whoa, hold on, *cara mia.* I was guessing. But I'm right, aren't I?"

All the fight went out of her. "How did you guess? I thought I hid my problems pretty well."

"Perhaps from most people, but I've been around a long time and I'm trained to be observant." He stroked her hair, soothing her with his touch. She found herself burrowing into his chest, seeking his strength.

"A long line of my ancestors had the same problem I do. At least that's what my mother says. She's got it too and she's lived longer than most, but she had me very young and has always been a bit healthier than I am. Most of the family tree I've been able to trace didn't live past about thirty-five, so I'm starting to worry about the future."

Ian wanted so badly to reassure her. If she truly were demi-vampir, he knew his brethren would do all they could to protect her and prolong her life. Such had been done in the past when creatures had been discovered who lived with one foot in both the mortal and immortal worlds. It was a cruel twist of fate that would allow a full vampire to find his mate, only to have a child that was not fully either mortal or vampire.

Most true mates underwent the conversion before having children. Only once in a rare while, tragedy struck, leaving the child and all their children for generations—as might well be the case with Jena—half and half.

But Ian needed to know for certain before he raised her hopes. He had to taste her blood. It was a deep-seated desire, both to satisfy his curiosity about her origins and perhaps offer protection, but also because he desired her more than any woman he had ever met in all his long years. She intrigued him on so many levels and had since the moment he'd first seen her.

"So what gave me away?" Her voice was small, her head resting just under his chin, against his chest. She was tired and wrung out emotionally after the rigors of the night, he could tell. He wanted nothing more than to ease her sadness and bring her joy. But first he had to convince her. He would force nothing from her. She would give—and give freely—he swore it by all he still held holy.

"The aversion to silver, the fair skin that probably burns easily. Your penchant for working the night shift. The lights on in your house at all hours of the night. Your excellent taste in wine." He rattled off the list, injecting a bit of humor into his voice. She needed a friend right now, but she would know how much he wanted her beneath him before too much more time had passed. He would choose his moment though, to ease her into the idea of becoming his lover. Such things had to be finessed in this day and age.

She chuckled and he felt it against his heart. Contrary to legend, Ian did have a heart and it still beat. His skin wasn't cold. No, his base temperature was actually a little hotter than a normal human, thanks to the changes that had been made to his blood and tissues on a cellular level when he'd been turned. The blood that flowed in his veins now was laced with a substance some claimed was not originally of this earth. It gifted him—or cursed, depending on your point of view—with immortal life and certain limitations, such as an inability to walk in the sun, eat food, or touch silver.

"You really want to get a taste of my blood?"

Ian sucked in a breath as she leaned back to look deep into his eyes. Slowly, he nodded.

"All right."

Was she saying yes? So much for finesse. It looked like the direct approach worked after all with this spectacular, unpredictable woman.

"But I want something in return."

Ian's exuberant joy was tempered by her words. He would give her anything, agree to any terms, if he could just have her essence, and with it her delectable body.

"What do you desire?" He knew the fire that flared in his veins flickered in his eyes as she touched him. She moved her hands up around his neck and into his hair, tugging downward.

"I want the fairytale, Ian. At least for tonight. I want this Valentine's Day to mean something more than disappointment and disillusionment. I want to make love to you all night long and feel like you really want to be here, with me, in my bed. I want to believe...just for a little while...that a man like you could actually want a girl like me. Just once, before I die."

Her words drilled into his core and nearly broke his heart. Ian drew her close against his chest, hugging her, and dipping his head to nuzzle her ear.

"I can give you that," he breathed into the delicate shell, "but *cara mia*, it won't be an illusion." She gasped as he bit down gently on her earlobe before trailing his lips down her neck. "I've wanted you since the moment I first saw you." He used one hand on her lower back to pull her softly rounded hips into his body, pressing his hard cock against her, rubbing insistently. "Feel what you do to me? It's been like this since the moment I first breathed in your delicate scent. You enchanted me that first night, *cara*, and I've dreamed of this every moment since."

"Ian," she gasped as he licked her throat. "Ian, kiss me. Please."

He growled low in his throat. Satisfaction tore through him at her breathy moan.

"Your wish," he dragged his lips up to hers, "is my command."

Careful of his lengthening incisors, Ian claimed the kiss he'd waited weeks to initiate. Never before had he wanted to drink in a woman and never let her go, but he felt that way with Jena. She was special to him already, and her taste flooded his senses with unbelievable fire. She was sweet and delicate, her shy tongue dueling with his after a little coaxing, setting him ablaze.

When his teeth nicked her lip, he drew back at her gasp.

The sight of the little red droplet forming on her plump inner lip was nearly his undoing, but he managed to control himself long enough to lean forward and lick it away with his tongue. He just couldn't resist.

That tiny taste was enough to send him reeling. She was a feast for the senses, her essence flooded him with power the likes of which he had never known before. Ian staggered back as her beautiful face scrunched up with concern for him.

"Ian?" Her hand went to his elbow, supporting him while she walked him into the living room. "What's wrong?"

He stopped her when she would have pushed him down to rest on her pretty flowered couch. He tugged her back into his arms, where she belonged, but allowed her concern to wash over him like a healing balm.

"Are you okay?"

"I've never been more alive, *cara mia*, not even since before I was turned." He knew a grin was splitting his face, but he couldn't contain his joy. Just that little taste told him all he needed to know about her origins. Her blood contained trace amounts of the substance that made his own blood so different—just in a slightly different form and in much lower concentration. She was truly half in his world and half in the mortal realm.

"Why are you looking at me so strangely?" She had a hesitant smile on her face that he longed to kiss away, but he had to share his good news with her first.

"It's your blood." Her hand immediately went to the scratch on her lip, her delicate finger tracing over the tiny wound. "Even from that tiny taste I can tell you are what we call demi-vampir, Jena. Somewhere in your family tree is one of my kind who mated with a mortal and produced one of your ancestors. It doesn't happen often, but every once in a while, something prevents true mates from completing the bond and even rarer, a child results who is like you, demi-vampir."

"What?" Ian could see the thoughts racing behind her eyes, her scientifically trained mind trying to grasp what he was saying. "Are you sure?"

"As certain as I can be. Jena, honey, this means that you won't have to fear dying young any longer. I, and my brethren, will protect you and nurture you. We can help you live a normal mortal life span, if that is your wish, or you can be easily changed. Legend even holds that a demi-vampir, once turned, still retains some ability to walk in the sun, among other things."

Her eyes narrowed in thought. "I don't know if I want to be a vampire, Ian. I mean, it's okay for my friends—they have someone to share eternity with—but for me alone? I'm just not sure about that at all."

"Well, you don't have to decide anything now, *cara*. All this means is that you can stop worrying about your future health. We know what afflicts you now and we can take steps to see you through the rough patches."

Ian was thrilled by the way she clung to him, burrowing into his chest as if she wanted to take up residence. But there were other things to see to this night. Pleasure being chief among them.

"Where's your bedroom, sweetheart?" He kept his voice pitched low, letting her know it was still her decision, giving her an out should she decide to withdraw.

Jena's beautiful eyes mesmerized him as she drew back to meet his gaze. Very deliberately, she looked to the doorway on his right and then back. Then she smiled a sexy, engaging smile as she pulled slightly back from him and led him by the hand to her room. She barely had the door closed behind them before he had her back in his arms.

Chapter Four

Jena could hardly believe what Ian had just told her. First, to learn that he truly desired her had been a naughty dream come true. If she were being brutally honest with herself, she'd admit that Ian had made her cream her panties the moment she first saw him...and every time since.

Then to feel his amazingly hot kiss. That kiss had nearly knocked her right off her feet. But she wouldn't have minded that at all, as long as Ian landed on top of her. She had to suppress a giggle of pure excitement as she led him into her bedroom. This was her inner sanctum, her place to retreat from the rigors of the day and dream of a man like the one who stood before her now.

She knew she couldn't keep him, but Ian was the stuff dreams were made of. His body was hard muscled and his gaze followed her every movement with an intensity that made her heart pound and her breath catch. It had been like that from the first. Ever since she'd met him, he'd starred in all her erotic flights of fancy. And tonight she would live them, one by one, for as long as he would allow it. This was her night. She vowed to make the most of it.

The bombshell he'd just dropped about her blood had nearly floored her, but Jena didn't want to think about it just then. It was enough to know that there was hope. Ian had given her that. He'd given her hope that her condition wouldn't be fatal quite as soon as it had been for her ancestors. And perhaps there was hope now for her mother as well. If the vampires were willing to help her, they would probably also be willing to help her mom. She'd have to ask Ian—later. First, there was the much more pressing matter of fulfilling a few dearly held fantasies.

"I want you so much, lass." Ian's dark voice breathed into the hair at her nape as his lips and tongue caressed her neck. "I want to hear you scream my name in pleasure as I come inside you and drink your sweet essence. I want to put my mark on you so you'll never forget me. Ever."

"Damn, Ian. When you play a part, you really take it all the way, don't you?" Oddly she felt a little cheated that his ardent words were just part of the fantasy she'd demanded from him. Suddenly she wished her words unsaid. She should have just let events unfold as they would. By asking for the dream, she'd made herself unsure if anything he said or did was real. She'd wonder all night, and for years to come, if the things he was saying were what he was really feeling or just what he thought she wanted to hear.

Jena stepped back, tugging out of his arms.

"What is it?" Immediately his hands cupped her shoulders, not allowing her to step away. "What's wrong?" His gentle voice sounded through her heart, cracking it open and finding its way within.

"Can you forget what I said earlier? I don't want you saying things tonight that you don't mean. I thought I did...but...I don't. Can we start over?"

Ian tugged her closer, his unexpected strength making her stumble just a tiny bit, but he was there to catch her with his hard body. He demanded her attention as fire leapt visibly in his eyes.

"I don't have to start over, *cara,* because I haven't said anything to you tonight that I didn't mean. I have never, and will never, lie to you."

"But—"

He placed one long finger over her lips, stilling her words. "You wanted me to pretend, but what you're getting is real. I don't have to pretend because I do want you—more than any woman I've ever known. I want to fuck you and feast on you 'til the sun parts us and then I want to come back for more tomorrow night. You'd better rest up and eat your Wheaties because you'll need your strength. I'm giving you fair warning right now."

"But how can you—?"

His lips stilled her worried words this time and when he drew back, she was his to command. His magnetism had always drawn her, but now focused on her exclusively, she could barely control herself. She was beyond caring if his words would prove false in the harsh light of morning when she was alone once more. For this moment, and the hours to come, she would suspend disbelief as much as she could and just enjoy the wonder of him.

"Make love to me, Ian."

He swept her up into his arms and placed her gently on the bed. Luckily it was large enough for both of them, though he was a tall man. The bed in his home was larger still, and he would introduce her to it as soon as possible, but for tonight, this first time, he would take her here, amidst the lace and frippery of her feminine retreat.

Another man might've been intimidated by the womanly surroundings, but Ian delighted in the idea that he was conquering her pretty rose colored bedroom just as he conquered her soft pink flesh. He wasted little time on her clothes, pulling her top off over her shoulders and tugging at her skirt. The front closure on her lacy bra gave way under his questing fingers and the thin cotton of her panties was no match for his decisive pull.

She was naked.

And so incredibly beautiful.

Ian was amazed she had such power over him. Her light skin called to him, her warm scent begged him to breathe her in and never let go. Gingerly, he touched her, cupping the smooth roundness of her breast, watching with genuine enjoyment as her nipple pebbled and strained upward in his hand, calling for his kiss.

He bent and licked the pointy tip, reveling in her sighs and the tender feel of her fingers sifting through the hair at the nape of his neck. She held him to her, encouraging him with her panting breaths and eager fingers as he sucked her nipple deep, using just a hint of the teeth that were even now lengthening to scrape along her delicate skin. He would leave no mark, but he would tantalize her in a way she'd never forget.

She would never forget him, or this night. He would see to it. It was a need deep inside him, to put his mark on this woman and brand her for life. He didn't question the need. It just was. And it was close to overwhelming.

Ian took a moment to rid himself of his clothes in short order, not leaving the bed. He knelt above her body, tearing at his shirt and throwing it across the room as her gaze followed his every movement. When his chest was bare, he lay back on the bed at her side, encouraging her exploration with a few nudges and a wicked smile. Jena didn't let him down.

Her little hands roamed over his chest as he tugged at his pants, finally succeeding at getting them off when she turned the tables on him. Her pouty lips circled his nipple and then that devilish tongue of hers peeped out to tease him, but he wouldn't let her have her way...this time.

No, this first time was all about getting inside her as fast as possible. The hunger was riding him hard and he knew he had little control left. If he wanted to make this good for her at all, he had to be in control of every movement.

He might give her a turn later at calling the shots, but not this time.

He flipped her onto her back and spread her legs, kneeling between them. She was open to him and very vulnerable in this position, but a quick check of her expression told him all he needed to know. She was with him.

"This time it's got to be fast, but I'll make it good, baby. I promise. I just can't wait."

"Don't wait, Ian." Her breathy sighs pushed him forward, his hard cock seeking its home between her slick thighs.

"I'm sorry, *cara*. I can't wait anymore. I need to be inside you."

And with a long, hot shove, he was home. Inside her. Welcomed into her depths with a feeling of warmth he'd seldom felt in his long life.

"Ian!" Jena wrapped her luscious legs around him, using her thigh muscles to pull him closer. Ian couldn't resist. He leaned down over her, capturing her lips with his in a kiss of heat and discovery as he began moving, powerful and sure, within her.

He pumped her slow and steady, now that he was where he wanted to be, he could take the time to make sure he was with her every step of the way. She was so responsive, it took little to make her climax, once and then again. She came so beautifully, her energy bathing his senses as he drew it all in.

Ian had fed off of many women in the centuries of his existence, but never had an orgasm given him such a feeling. It made him want more. And more.

Ian drove steadily, delighting in the feel of her pussy clamped around him, her inner muscles milking him as he moved faster and faster. The fire was overtaking him, drowning him in the heat of her sexy body and he was a willing victim. Her orgasm rippled through him yet again, recharging his psi energies and pushing him onward.

Ian rubbed his chest along her soft body, loving the feel of her tightened nipples as they rasped over his skin. She was so soft, so delicate, yet so explosive in his arms. She was perfect.

Only one thing would make this experience even better.

Her blood.

Ian licked his way up her neck to the pulse he could feel pounding just under the surface. He could just hear the faint sound of her heart, tempting him as it pumped her rich blood through the network of veins and arteries he knew so well. All it would take was a sip. Just a taste of her amazing demi-vampir blood.

He had to guard against taking too much. He didn't want to hurt her and he knew with such passion flowing, he could easily get carried away. No, he'd have to be very, very careful.

Just a taste. That's all he wanted. He needed to taste her essence as he came inside her lovely body. It was imperative.

Leaning in, he licked over the spot he chose, just over her pulse.

"Give it to me now, *cara*," he ordered in a soft voice, just beneath her ear. "Now I make you mine."

"I'm yours, Ian. Yours!"

Her whispered words spurred him on as he bit down as gently as he could manage. At the first taste of her flowing blood, he knew.

He came hard inside her tight channel, flooding her womb with his seed as her essence flooded his mouth and senses. Senses that were screaming at him in triumph.

She was his.

Jena thought she knew what to expect from a vampire's bite after the experience with Sebastian, but Ian's slow, sexy sucking was nothing like what Sebastian had done to her. It was also nothing like anything she had remotely imagined or dreamed.

It was better.

And more intimate.

She felt him in the marrow of her bones...and in her mind.

Ian?

Oh, dear God in heaven! His words sounded through her mind differently than before. This time she didn't just hear his words, but she felt his wonder, his amazement, his humility and joy. It stole her breath as she peaked yet again under the triple assault of his hot, hard cock, his sucking mouth, and his overwhelming feelings of awe.

She picked up more than that as his climax began to ease. She heard the words and saw the images of his life. She shared in his past and realized dimly that he was doing the same. He was in her mind!

Ian!

I'm here, my love. I'm here now and I'll never leave. We'll never be apart ever again.

Oh, God, Ian. What is this?

Don't you know? Can't you see it in my memories? Can't you feel my hopes come to fruition, my prayers of eight hundred years answered in a single moment? He drew back and stared down into her eyes. She saw herself reflected there. It was an odd sensation, but it felt so...right.

Are you trying to tell me—?

You're my one and only. My mate. The one woman in all the world, and all the centuries, who can complete me. Don't you feel it? Don't you feel me within you, a part of you, in every possible way? He stroked his long cock gently inside her, reminding her of his presence not only in her mind, but in her body as well. *I love you, Jena. More than life. And I will love you to the end of my existence.*

Oh, Ian! She clutched his shoulders, tears leaking from her eyes, but they were tears of joy. She felt the truth of his words, felt his emotions as he felt them, as she guessed he was feeling hers.

Ian kissed her nose, then licked away her tears. *That's right, my love. I feel what you feel, just as you feel what I feel. Isn't it fantastic?*

Amazing. It's amazing, Ian. I never realized... She trailed off as she got caught up in his emotions, just scratching the surface of his memories of the seemingly endless years he'd searched in vain for her. His wonder at finding her was off the charts and it humbled her to think this magnificent man—this knight of old—could be so thrilled with the idea of having plain old her in his life. *Oh, Ian. I love you too. So much!*

I know. The cocky arrogance was back, but she could feel the sentiment and indulgent love behind his words. He was such a special man. And she was his mate. The idea would take some getting used to, but she didn't mind that one bit. She'd love delving into this man's mind, his heart, and his incredible sexual expertise. After all, she had a lot of catching up to do!

"Hold that thought, love. First we have to secure the room against the sun and then I'm going to barricade the door, take the phone off the hook and spend as much time as I possibly can making love to you."

Chapter Five

Ian pulled swiftly from her body and went over to close the heavy drapes, inspecting them for light fastness. She could hear his thoughts and he apparently *heard* her too when she told him the curtains were indeed sun proof. She'd had them made specially since her skin had always been so fair and she couldn't spend a lot of time in the sun.

Ian returned to her moments later. He rested his broad back against the headboard of her full size bed and nestled her into his arms, resting his chin lightly over the crown of her head. She sighed and snuggled against his warmth, feeling him taking up residence in her heart and very soul.

"I can hardly believe this is happening. I mean, when Sebastian saved Christy in the hospital, it was a shock to learn that vampires existed, but then I found out about Lissa and Kelly. I never dared dream I'd be a match too."

Ian seemed to ponder her words. "I know some of our researchers were already looking into why and how the three of them congregated together as such close friends. Finding a cluster of mates so close like that seemed statistically impossible before, but now, after finding you and knowing your true nature, it begins to make more sense."

She shifted a bit in his arms to look up at him. "How so?"

"Your power probably drew them, my love." He leaned down and kissed her sweetly, then pulled back again. "Even demi-vampir have some echo of the true vampire's influence. Fate plays a role too, of course, but I'm not surprised those three women—destined to become vampire mates—would be drawn into your orbit. Tell me," he stroked her shoulder and down her back, "were any of them friends before they met you?"

Jena had to think back. "Christy was my roommate and I introduced her to the others. I met Carly, Lissa and Kelly in calculus class and we formed a study group. I don't think they knew each other before that, but they've been as close as sisters ever since." She resettled her cheek against his warm chest, just above the reassuring beat of his heart. "I met Sally about a year later in a martial arts class and she just jelled with the rest of the group even though she's a bit older than the rest of us. After that, the group of us were pretty inseparable, even though we were majoring in different things."

"It's as I thought then. You are the link that drew those women together. I wonder—"

"If Sally is also some vampire's mate?" She finished the thought for him. "Now wouldn't that be a kicker? Especially considering her line of work. Sensible cops like Sally probably don't deal well with the supernatural."

"You might be surprised." Ian turned her, teasing her skin with the light dusting of chest hair that rubbed her in all the right ways. "It's a matter that definitely should be explored—but later. Right now I want to make love to my beautiful mate once more before the sun rises."

"Ian, do you think—?"

"That your potent demi-vampir blood will allow me to walk in the sun?" He shrugged but there was an almost painful mix of hope and resignation in his eyes. "We shall see. But I dare not get my hopes up. We'll take this slow. The first step, which we'll take tomorrow night, will be to notify Marc LaTour, the Master of this region, about our mating and your family history. I trust him. He'll help us figure out how to protect you."

"Protect me?"

"Honey, if word of your demi-vampir nature gets out, every unscrupulous vampire in the world will be looking to bite you. The idea of seeing the sun again is very tantalizing. Even if your blood doesn't work like that, just the idea that it *might,* will bring them flocking to your door."

"Can't we just keep it a secret? I mean, I've lived this long without any problems. As long as we don't tell anybody, I can probably continue living as I have."

He paused, seeming to consider her words. "Yes, that's true, and I definitely do want to keep it a secret as much as we can, but we have to tell Marc. For one thing, it's my duty. For another, we'll need his help to establish protection for your mother. And for yet another," he lay down facing her on the wide bed, "we might be able to use this to our advantage, for the protection of both vampires and mortals alike. If I do gain some ability to move about when the rest of my kind cannot, it could be a major advantage. One that the Master Vampire will need to know about in order to utilize."

"Hmm, that's my man. Always the soldier." She stroked his tightly muscled shoulders. "I trust your judgment, Ian, but I'll admit I'm a little scared of all this."

He kissed her deeply, then pulled back. "I won't let any harm come to you, my love. It would literally kill me if anything happened to you."

"You know that goes both ways, don't you?" She stroked his cheek. "It's so odd. I've only really just gotten to know you, but you're in my heart already. I *know* you, Ian."

"That's the way it is between destined mates—or so I've heard. You can talk to your friends about it now. They'll tell you it's how it's meant to be." He moved over her as he spoke, his words trailing across her skin in little, warm puffs of air. "But we have time now. Time to learn each other and love each other. I know I'm looking forward to it. Almost as much as I'm looking forward to coming inside you a few more times before this night is through."

Jena all but purred at his words, shifting under him in welcome. "I think that could be arranged."

Ian paused, staring down into her eyes intently. "You feed something in my soul that no one ever has, Jena. You are my world."

"Oh, Ian." She battled the tears that wanted to form behind her eyes, her love for this special man welling up inside her, nearly out of control. He felt it of course, just as she felt the steady wonder of his words through their connection. She was so much a part of him now. She couldn't explain it and understanding it was beyond her at the moment, but they were joined in more than just the obvious way. "I love you."

His lips claimed hers then as his body covered hers. His weight was welcome, though he used his forearms to brace most of his heavy bulk off her. Still, the tantalizing brush of his chest, the rasp of his legs over and between hers, all these things only heightened her pleasure.

Ian felt what she felt. Her pleasure heightened his own in a way he had never before experienced. So this is what his newly mated friends had discovered. The perfect union of souls, the communion of spirits that brought more fulfillment than anything he'd ever known. He could happily live on this abundant, exuberant energy for the rest of his life and never go hungry.

If Jena would let him.

If she chose to stay demi-vampir and never be converted to full vampire, he would live out her lifespan with her and leave this realm with her when she departed. It was just that simple. He could not live without her and would follow when she moved on to other realms.

Jena stopped his shower of kisses with her gentle palms on either side of his head, pushing upward to get his attention. When their eyes met, he knew she'd walked in his thoughts and not liked what she found there.

He tried to head off her serious words. "I'm sorry. Let's not ruin this moment with thoughts of the future, my love. It was wrong of me to dwell on such thing at a moment like this."

He saw as well as felt her think on his words as he rubbed his lower half against hers, reigniting the fire he'd let flag. Her hands tugged downward now, bringing his lips within a breath of hers.

"Don't let it happen again, lover. We'll talk about that other stuff...when the time comes. But not now." She trailed her lips over his, her lower body reaching upwards as if yearning for him. And he felt the deep need in her thoughts that reflected his own.

All that mattered now was this, their coming together in passion and...love. For the first time in his long life, he'd found a woman who loved him and he loved her in return. It didn't seem possible that he could be so blessed, but he didn't question it. No, the time for questions was over. Now was a time for action.

"Later," he agreed as he moved his lips down her body, stopping here and there to worship at her soft spots. "We'll talk later."

He paused for a long time at her breasts, toying with her ripe nipples, teasing them with his teeth in a way that made her squirm deliciously. He felt her responses and he used his own mental powers to influence her reactions, to increase her sexual fire. He made her come just from his lips on her body, loving the little climax that fueled his own ardor. She was so responsive to him, it was gratifying to feel the love along with the passion for once. It was a heady mix that fueled him more than he ever would have thought. Love tasted divine to his senses and he wanted more.

His goal for the evening became clear. He would keep her coming for him all night long. Ian smiled wolfishly as he thought of the orgy of the senses to come. By morning, neither of them would be able to walk. He'd be completely drunk on their power, and she would be blissfully exhausted.

"Mmm," she wiggled deliciously under him as he moved lower, "I like your plan, Ian."

He started, knowing she'd just read his thoughts as easily as if they were her own. Perhaps she was even unaware of doing so. It felt so natural, even now, he was just barely aware of her warm presence in his mind as he was in hers. She was comfortable, and so very welcome. His heart poured love into their connection, and she smiled at him so serenely he felt overwhelmed by the power this small demi-vampir woman had over him. Still, he wouldn't have it any other way. He would rather have one night with her, than all his centuries alone.

But he was getting maudlin again and he had an objective. One from which they would both reap the benefits, should he achieve his orgasmic goal.

Ian scooted lower on the bed, spreading her legs wide as he settled between them. She was open to his gaze and she was devastatingly beautiful to him.

Even though he had pleasured many, many women over his centuries, it had been a long time indeed since he'd taken any real time to fully immerse himself in his lover as he so badly wanted to do with Jena. He wanted to worship every inch of her skin, pay homage to every freckle and tiny scar. He wanted to learn her body and study every dip and valley he held so dear. The lesson would begin tonight and last for years, and he would be a diligent student.

And he would teach her a few things as well. For all that she had lovers in the past, Ian could easily read her responses, and memories for that matter, to know that Jena still had quite a bit to learn about giving and receiving pleasure. He would be a dutiful master. And she'd love every minute of his tutelage.

The fingers of one hand teased her nipples as his mouth hovered, breathing hot air down over the sensitive folds of her sex. His other hand spread her pussy wide as he lowered his lips to kiss her softly at first, then with more fervor.

Her taste was divine. Her scent and feel was all that was right in the universe, and he never wanted to be parted from her again. This was *his* woman. The one created just for him. Fate had brought them together and he would allow nothing and no one to part them ever again. It was his destiny to protect and cherish his mate. And love her. Oh, how he loved every last thing about her. He would spend lifetimes proving his love and exploring the amazing new feelings she brought out in him.

Ian had always considered himself a hard man, but when confronted by Jena's soft heart and commanding personality, he found himself as pliable as clay. She could shape him into anything she chose, and he would conform gladly, but he knew she was well aware of her power over him and her soul was too pure to use it against him. Her love for him would prevent her from ever hurting him, just as his love for her did the same. Together they were invincible. Each would protect the other. Forever.

Or how ever long they had.

Ian growled at himself, knowing he was heading into dangerous territory with his thoughts again. He refocused instead on the wondrous taste of his mate. His. Mate.

Never had he thought he would speak those words, but here she was, just where he wanted her—spread wide and waiting for his possession. He exerted a little mental push and sucked on her distended clit, teasing it a little with his tongue.

"Ian!"

He loved the sound of his name on her lips when she came.

He shifted back, lifting her up and flipping her onto her stomach. Running his large hands over the pale globes of her heart-shaped ass, he marveled at the perfection the fates had gifted him with. She was gorgeous.

And her ass would look even better after a bit of his loving discipline.

"Ian?" Her voice quavered as she jumped a bit, quite obviously reading his thoughts.

He bent to kiss the small of her back as his hands massaged her butt cheeks with a circular motion.

"Don't be afraid. I'd never hurt you."

"But...but you want to spank me?" She sounded lovingly confused as he nipped her fleshy cheek with just slightly distended fangs, though he was careful not to break the skin.

"You've never been spanked by a lover." He didn't ask it as a question, he could read it in her memories. "Never played the truly submissive role."

"No." Her reply was breathless and he could read excitement and the desire to try in her mind. Deep down, this beautiful, capable woman wanted to be submissive to her lover. She just hadn't known it and had never found a man strong enough to do it. Ian had no doubts about his ability to lovingly master her pleasure, though he would never try to dominate her in daily life. Still, he was just barbarian enough to want to take the lead in the bedroom—or wherever they made love—and if he was reading her right, she was more than willing to submit.

"Could God have given me a more perfect mate? I think not." Ian chuckled as he raised her arms above her head. "Don't move your hands now. Keep them just where I put them."

"Okay." Her voice was shaky with both excitement and a hint of anxiety. He noted the way her little fingers curled into the bedding, scratching and straining with her rising anticipation.

He kissed the nape of her neck, loving that she was unsure, but willing to trust him. He loved her. Period. He let that thought flow through their connection and was gratified when she relaxed a bit under his hands. He stroked down her back, enjoying the soft feel of her skin against his rough hands. He kneaded her tense muscles, giving her an impromptu back rub that went down her legs and back up to the fleshy globes of her ass...and between.

One hand dipped into the dark recesses between her legs as his other hand arranged her long limbs, spreading them wider to accommodate his searching touch. She rewarded him with a sigh of delight as his fingers slid home within her tight channel, testing her wetness. She was so ready for him, but he had one more thing to show her before he took his pleasure.

Holding the fingers of one hand deep within her, he used his other hand to swat her ass. It wasn't a light blow, but neither would it do any injury. The stinging swat made her jump, but he kept his fingers within her, riding her throughout. He loved the way she clenched on his hand and would give anything for her to do the same on his cock.

Patience, he counseled himself. He'd get there in time. First he had to be sure she was okay with this and that she'd enjoy it as much as he did.

He delivered a few more stinging spanks, loving the way she responded, crying out his name on excited sobs. He also noted the lovely pinkening of her ass cheeks. They were as beautiful as he'd imagined and more, with her amazing blood rushing to the surface to soothe her stinging skin.

"You like that?" He nearly had to bite his lip to keep from chuckling. She was on fire in his arms, as responsive as he could've hoped. She was most definitely enjoying this little game and it was only the first of many he had to teach her. Sex between them would only get better—and more adventurous—with time. Ian looked forward to it with glee.

"Ian!" She nearly came as he delivered another blow, but he held her back from the precipice, removing his fingers from her wet channel as she cried out in protest. But he wanted to be inside her when she came this time, and he wanted to come with her—deep, hard and buried in his mate.

Moving quickly, he stuffed a pillow beneath her hips, raising them just a bit, and took his place behind her, between her spread legs. Shoving home, he impaled her on his cock in one smooth move as she bucked upward and nearly screamed with satisfaction. He was so hard and ready, he would come very quickly, but then she was just as close, so it would all be okay.

Urgently, he moved within her, sliding in and out, establishing a torturous rhythm that drove them both higher. He held her hips and watched the way her miraculous body accepted him. She was so special, so alluring, so ultimately feminine to him. She was all he'd ever wanted and all he would ever want.

And she was all his.

She accepted his quirks and was willing to learn. He liked that in a woman, but he *loved* it in *his* woman. He made sure that thought communicated through to her as he plowed more forcefully into her welcoming sheath. His hands massaged her pink cheeks and tugged on her hips, getting a little rougher as they both neared the edge.

Ian placed a single, strategic swat on her sweet ass that made her tighten on him in a way that could not be ignored. Collapsing down over her back, Ian sank his teeth—now fully distended—into the curve of her neck, allowing just a hint of her sweet essence to coat his tongue as he drove them both over the edge.

It didn't take much.

His mate's blood was far more powerful than any other's. Her orgasm powered through his soul in a way he'd never felt before and would never feel again with any other woman.

Only her.

For all eternity.

Or as long as she would give them.

After a long, long, satisfying climax, Ian began to relax. She had wrung him out and as predicted, he was more than a little drunk on the energy that came of their joining.

He grunted a little as he moved off her, taking his weight from her in an effort not to crush her. She was so precious to him, so fragile...so mortal, regardless that she was demi-vampir. He would spend the rest of his life seeing to her health and safety regardless of her decision, though he hoped and prayed she would choose to spend eternity with him, exploring their love.

Ian rearranged their limbs when he found the energy to move again so that she rested against him, spooned into his body. Where she belonged. She was already fast asleep, and he couldn't love her more.

Chapter Six

Ian stared at his lover's beautiful face as he felt dawn break in the east. For centuries, the creeping light of dawn had been his signal to seek shelter away from the damaging light of the sun. It had sapped him of energy and sent him into a sleep that was as close to death as he could come. Only dire circumstances had been able to rouse him when the sun ruled the sky, and then only to a semi-conscious state.

But Ian greeted this new dawn with more vigor than he'd ever felt. It sizzled through his veins in a dance of glory, though he counseled himself silently to not get his hopes up. A few sips of demi-vampir blood might give him a boost in energy, but it didn't necessarily mean he'd be able to go sunbathing anytime soon.

Though Ian would sacrifice a great deal to just be able to glimpse the earth bathed in sunlight one more time, he would not risk the new happiness he'd found with Jena. Joined as they were now, if one of them felt pain, the other would too, and the bond would only grow and deepen over time. They were one now, never to be apart again in this realm.

It was his greatest joy. Greater even than the fantastical, forbidden idea of seeing the sun again after over eight hundred years.

"Mmm, what time is it?" Jena's groggy voice reached his ears as he contemplated their future.

"Dawn."

Jena sat up, wiping sleep from her eyes. "I need a shower."

Ian pulled her into his arms and kissed the top of her disheveled hair. "I love how you look, all rumpled from making love with me."

Jena chuckled and pushed away. "You're sweet, but I'm a wreck." She pulled at the sheets, trying to disentangle herself. "Ew, and so is this bed." Jena stood and pulled the sheets off, tossing them to the floor as she headed toward the attached bathroom. "There are clean sheets on the top shelf of the closet if you want to freshen up the place a bit. If not, I'll do it when I get out of the shower." She stopped by the bathroom door, her hand on the knob. "You do want to sleep here with me today, right?"

She looked so lovely, standing there, gloriously rumpled and nude, her body showing every sign of their loving the night before. Her thighs were slippery with their cum, her nipples and other soft spots pink from his attentions.

Ian couldn't stay away from her.

He moved across the room and swept her into his arms, kissing her deeply. When he pulled back, she was dazed and breathless, just the way he liked her.

"I wouldn't dream of leaving you today, my love." His words were spoken softly into the shell of her ear. "Or any other day."

"Ian!" She spasmed in his arms as he moved her up against the bathroom door, lifted her legs and wrapped them swiftly around his waist. Sparing only a moment to make certain she was ready, he pushed into her, joining them yet again in a fast and furious fuck up against the bathroom door.

He moved hard against her, unable to take his time now that he had his woman in his arms and his cock where it most wanted to be. His arms supported her light weight as she surrendered to his mastery, crying out as he plunged deeper and deeper into her tight, wet heat.

This wasn't the torrid, teasing loving of the night before. No, this was even more primal. This was a claiming, a marking, a statement of ownership. And it worked both ways.

Never before had a woman owned a piece of his heart or been part of his soul. Never before had he found himself so lost in a woman, he ceased to be aware of the rising sun. Never before had he needed to come inside his partner so badly, it was a physical ache.

Ian felt he balls tighten the moment before he bit down on her neck, sipping lightly, knowing he'd been rough with his teeth the night before and wanting to at least make that up to her while his cock pummeled her pussy from below. But Jena was with him. She was crying out with every thrust, trying to move with him even though he held all the power in this position. She urged him on with her tightening inner muscles, holding him when he withdrew and clamping down on him when he slid home.

As his teeth pierced her flesh and the amazing taste of her blood blossomed on his tongue, he thrust within her sheath one last time, holding tight as he came in a rush. She climaxed once more, with him, screaming low in her throat like a jungle cat, milking his cock with her spasming walls as he drank of her essence and filled her with his seed.

Ian licked her neck, sealing the small wounds as Jena wound down from that incredibly fast peak. She held him with arms that felt like limp spaghetti, unsure if her legs would even support her after that amazing, continuous orgasm.

"Oh, baby. I think I'm going to like being with you if that's what I get first thing each morning." She sent him a lascivious smile and winked as he drew back, rewarded when he chuckled and kissed her playfully on the nose. He needed to laugh more and she was just the woman to see to it.

"I'd give it to you morning, noon and night, if I could."

"Hmm." She licked the seam of his lips, sidetracked to his stubbly jaw as she kissed her way to his ear, sucking the lobe into her mouth briefly. "So what time is it now?"

He seemed to still, his muscles tensing a bit though he continued to hold her.

"You know something? I don't know." He spoke as if this was some kind of big news and Jena drew back to study his shocked expression. He met her gaze and a smile started in his own. "I'm always aware of the position of the sun somewhere in the back of my mind, but you just blew it all to hell and back. I have no idea what time it is."

"Well," she raised up just a tiny bit to look over his shoulder at the bedside table and the alarm clock that rested there, "what would you say if I told you it was almost eight o'clock in the morning?"

"Damn." The single word was laced with awe. "I've never felt this good—this awake—so late in the morning. My body's usually shutting down by now."

He let her legs slide down toward the floor, but retained his grip on her so she wouldn't fall. She was grateful for his support. She'd melted into a puddle after that last orgasm and wasn't quite recovered enough to stand on her own just yet.

"So my blood packs a punch then?"

He swooped down to give her a smooching kiss. “Undoubtedly. But it’s more than your blood. It’s you, Jena. It’s the love between us that heightens everything when we come together.” He kissed her softly, lovingly. “Let’s take that shower, then spend the rest of the day in bed.”

“Oh, I like that plan.” She pecked him on the cheek, then turned in his arms as he stepped back to allow her to open the bathroom door.

But she’d forgotten the window.

The bathroom window was wide open. And the sunlight was streaming in, dappling the sunny yellow shower curtain and sending shafts across the matching bath mat and towels in the towel rack. She heard a gasp from behind her and moved to shut the door, but Ian stayed her arm.

“Ian?” She turned to look at him. He was frozen in place, his eyes watering, but whether in pain or something else, she wasn’t sure. She felt within to see if she could use their new connection to learn what was going on, but all she could sense was shock and wonder laced with agony. “Ian, let me shut the door.”

“No. It’s okay.”

“But it’s hurting you!”

He pulled her into his arms. “Only a little.” He kissed her cheek. “Only a little. My God!” He squeezed her tight and she felt the wetness of his tears roll over her skin as he held her close. “My love, you’ve given me the greatest gift anyone could ever give. After eight hundred years of darkness, you’ve given me the light.”

Chapter Seven

With some experimentation, they discovered that Jena's blood gave Ian the ability to withstand some small amounts of sunshine, which was more than he'd ever been able to do before. He was like a child, wanting to see and do everything—testing his limits at every possible moment. Jena had to hold him back, often distracting him with sex as a way to keep him out of danger and safe in her bed. Where he belonged.

It was a good trade off. She knew he was aware of her ploy, but he humored her and pleasured them both in the process. It was a truly win-win situation.

The only difficult part for her was when they visited Kelly and Marc LaTour's home the night after they'd first joined. Kelly was one of her best friends, of course, but Marc had always been a little frightening to her. He was the Master Vampire of the region and had held that position for quite a long time. The man was so imposing, the only time Jena saw his icy demeanor thaw at all was when Kelly was near.

When his new wife was nearby, it was clear how much he loved her and that made him somewhat more human, though he was still a little scary. Jena knew she was welcome in their home, but in truth, she hadn't visited too many times since

Kelly and Marc's wedding. Kelly had been turned in a very violent way, but it was clear Marc loved her with every breath in his body.

When Ian and Jena stepped over the LaTour's threshold that night, their hosts seemed to know right away that something was very different.

"Good Lord." Marc's calm voice cut through the tense silence as all four of them faced each other. "And then there were four." Ian burst out laughing at Marc's cryptic words while the women shared confused looks.

Ian settled his arm around her shoulders and pulled her in close to his side. "Jena is my One, but that isn't the end of our news. We'll require the private room to relay the rest."

"That serious?" Marc's aristocratic eyebrow rose. He'd been an English nobleman before being turned to vampirism and he still reverted to his old mannerisms every now and again.

Ian nodded grimly as the four of them moved off toward the back of the house. There was a set of stairs leading downward and Kelly took Jena's hand for a quick squeeze as Marc led the way downward to a room Jena had never seen before. He flicked a bunch of switches and sealed the heavy door shut before speaking again.

"Okay. We're secure. Now what's so earth shattering that we had to come all the way down here?" Marc turned on them, all business, but with just a tiny glint of humor in his dark eyes.

"Jena is demi-vampir and this morning I saw sunlight for the first time in eight hundred years."

The silence in the room was deafening.

"Good Lord!" Marc collapsed into a chair while Kelly stared, probably receiving information by taking a walk through her mate's memories, Jena realized.

Jena started to feel very uncomfortable at being the center of such attention, but Kelly reached out, coming over and giving her a big hug. Kelly was a good friend and that hadn't changed after she'd been turned. Kelly still had a generous heart and probably always would. It was just the way she was wired.

"I'm so glad you've found love, sweetie. I wish Ian and you every happiness."

"Thanks, Kel." Jena truly loved her friend and was glad she was there. She had so many questions to ask her now that they each had a vampire mate in common. There was so much to learn.

"Now what about your mother?" Kelly pulled back with a friendly smile. "I bet she's like you, huh?"

"There's another one?" Marc's voice sounded behind Kelly.

Ian nodded, filling Marc in on the particulars. Marc's decisiveness impressed Jena as he immediately made plans with Ian to see to her mother's safety. It turned out, they both knew a very experienced enforcer named Julian who was near enough to her mother's home in New York to go and watch over her. Marc made the call from a secure phone and set the wheels in motion, swearing the enforcer to secrecy. Both men vouched for Julian when Jena sought their reassurances, but Ian's word was good enough for her.

She took a moment to sift through just a few of his memories—a skill she was getting better at as time went on—to get a better idea of what this Julian guy was all about. One thing she was able to learn from Ian's memories was that Julian was a very handsome man. Her mother would have to watch out with a hunk like that watching over her every move.

Marc asked Jena to call her mother and warn her about Julian's arrival. Jena didn't really relish the idea of breaking all her news to her mother in front of witnesses, but she knew the phone line, at least on this end, was secure. There was no real reason to think her mother might be in danger...yet. But if somehow word got out about her demi-vampir state, that could change in a hurry. The idea truly frightened her but Ian reached out and squeezed one of her hands, pouring comfort and confidence through their link and she felt reassured as she dialed her mother's number.

The call went about as well as could be expected. Jena's mom, Lillian, had a kind of radar where she was concerned and wanted to hop the next flight out to see her, but Jena convinced her to stay put. She told her about Ian—and Julian's imminent arrival—and Lillian jumped to all sorts of motherly conclusions that had her laughing out loud. That seemed, perversely, to reassure her mother and they rang off with a promise to call again the next day.

"Well?" Kelly wanted to know as Jena hung up the phone, still smiling and shaking her head. She looked up at her friend and chuckled.

"My mom is now convinced that I'm mixed up with the mafia."

Chapter Eight

Over the next week or two, Jena managed to convince her mother that Ian was *not* a member of the *Cosa Nostre.* Apparently the handsome Julian had more influence than Jena would have credited. Her mother had always been an eminently sensible woman, but when she mentioned Julian's name there was a certain wistfulness that communicated itself even over three thousand miles of telephone line.

They'd made plans to get together. Julian was flying her out on his private plane, in fact, which made Jena start to wonder just how rich this band of vampires she was now involved with was. Ian was playful when she broached the subject, teasing her about being a gold-digger, but he knew she wasn't. She could read that reassuring truth in his thoughts.

She was getting better and better at sifting through his amazing memories, and knew he was reading her life story just as she was doing with him. He smiled indulgently at her when he caught her at it, often hugging her close and distracting her with kisses and nips that turned into bites and very nice orgasms.

They were getting better at that too. They made love everywhere in her little house, then moved to Ian's more secure home so he could spend the day in complete safety. Sometimes she had to go to work, and she hated the separation as much as she knew he did, but they were joined so fully now, all she had to do was think of him and he was there, in her mind.

The feeling was incredibly comforting. Of course, he played little games too, turning her on with his words and the lascivious images he would send to her, all while she was at work with no way to ease the ache he stirred in her. She teased him back, though, and gave almost as good as she got.

One night, she was working the late shift when Ian started his teasing and she turned the tables. Ten minutes later, he locked her in her small office at the hospital, drew the shades and spread her wide on the edge of her desk. His cock was surging into her before she could even utter a protest. He could move unnaturally fast when the need arose.

Only after he'd seated himself within her tight depths did he allow her to speak.

"Know what happens when you tease the beast, sweetheart?" He forged into her as one hand held her hips, the other plucking hard at her nipples.

Jena shook her head in answer to his teasing question.

"You get bitten." He licked over her sensitive neck, preparing her.

Jena cried out. "Harder, Ian!" She tried to keep her voice low, but knew she was getting a little carried away. Ian always had that effect on her.

He answered her pleas, stroking in deep with each thrust until she was moaning against his chest, propped up by his strong arms. Her legs wrapped around his waist, claiming him as he moved his head down to kiss her lips. He trailed down her chin to her throat, sinking his fangs in deep as he thrust her to completion.

Ian was only a moment behind as he sipped at her amazing blood, licking her and relishing the essence of the one woman in all the world who could complete him. He was facing the door when he lifted his head, his cock still spurting within his woman. He licked his lips, knowing they were stained with her rich, red blood, and caught a flicker of movement out of the corner of his eye.

The door was open only a sliver, but it was enough for Ian to see the Dick on the other side, spying on them. Doctor Dick Schmidt let the door close, but not before Ian got a good look at him. The piss-ant was a voyeur, it seemed, and he'd gotten an eyeful.

Ian pulled out and cleaned up a bit, helping Jena set herself to rights. He kissed her softly as he made sure she could stand on her own.

"Will you be all right? There's something I have to take care of."

Jena nodded weakly, sinking down into her leather executive chair. She looked thoroughly fucked and Ian had to suppress the grin of satisfaction seeing her this way always gave him.

"Where are you going?"

Ian sighed. He didn't want her to know that he planned to silence the other man. By death, if necessary.

"Doctor Dick saw us. The little pervert must've unlocked your door and was peeking inside when I saw him."

"I gave him a key for emergencies. Not to spy on me!" Though she flushed with embarrassment, her words were practical as she drew in a calming breath. "What are you going to do to him?"

"Anything I have to."

Silence reigned for a moment before she stood and straightened her skirt. "I'll go with you. We should check his office first. It's two floors up."

Ian said not a word as she led the way to Dick Schmidt's office. When they arrived it was to find the good doctor dialing furiously as he clutched a small parchment-colored business card in one hand.

"Put down the phone." Ian put all the influence he could into his voice. The doctor struggled against the command, but the phone settled into its cradle as Ian moved forward. He was pleased to note Jena closing and locking the door to the office behind them. Ian plucked the card out of Dick's hand and glanced at it before tucking it into his pocket for further study. He knew the name well. Benjamin Steel was one of the few *Altor Custodis* agents Ian had been able to identify in this state, though he knew there were more. There had to be.

It was significant that Ben had given Dick his card. Could the *Altor Custodis* already know of Jena's bloodlines? Probably. That ancient sect had watched and tracked supernaturals through more centuries than Ian had lived. They were probably watching Jena and her mother as well, which was as comforting as it was frightening. They watched and recorded, but they probably wouldn't lift a finger to help if either of them were truly in danger. Ian began to wonder if the silver bracelet Dick had tried to give Jena on Valentine's Day was more sinister than he'd originally thought. Had it been a test of some sort? Did Dick know or suspect what she was?

"Fucking vampire!" Dick accused in a wobbly voice. Ian turned his full attention back to the matter at hand. That certainly answered some of his questions. Ian shook his head and made a tsking noise.

"I honestly didn't think you had any imagination whatsoever, Dick. I can't say I'm glad to find out I was wrong." Ian tugged Jena close to his side, tucking her under his arm. It was an obvious claim of ownership that wasn't lost on the sniveling mortal man. Ian nearly laughed aloud when Dick's chin rose stubbornly.

"Get away from her. You scum-sucking vampire!" Dick actually reached for his pocket and came up with a small cross he proceeded to wave at him. Luckily it was made of gold, not silver. Little did the mongrel know Ian had been a devout Catholic all his long life. Crosses—as long as they were not made of silver—held no fear for him. In fact, they represented the God he'd sworn his life to many times over since he'd been born all those centuries ago.

But Dick was starting to really piss him off.

Ian put Jena behind him and turned to snarl at the other man, baring his fangs and allowing the fire to creep into his eyes. He knew it made him look like a demon, and perhaps that's what he needed in this case. A little show of otherworldly strength might help him take the measure of this man he had previously underestimated.

"Back off, doctor. I won't warn you again."

The hand holding the cross shook as Ian stalked forward. Gently, almost reverently, he took the cross from Dick's trembling hands and kissed it with respect before placing it aside, safely out of harm's way. It really was a beautiful piece, heavy with age and many blessings that sent soothing energy through Ian when he touched it.

Perhaps that was the reason he felt pity for the sniveling man. Perhaps it was the reminder of his faith that stayed his hand when he could so easily have killed the good doctor.

Knowledge of his kind could not be allowed to spread. It was their most sacred law and one he'd vowed to uphold.

Or perhaps his rare compassion was spurred on by the soft, feminine voice of love in his mind.

Don't hurt him, Ian.

Ian sighed as he used his considerable mental powers to overcome Dick's weak mind. The man slumped to the floor in a heap, unconscious. He turned frustrated eyes to his mate briefly.

"He knows, Jena. That's not something I can ignore. Our law says he has to be contained."

"Killed, you mean," she scoffed. "Look, Ian. Regardless of how I feel about him personally, he is a good doctor. He saves a lot of lives. It would be a shame to lose his talent in the world when there are so many sick people who need his skill. Isn't there something you can do?"

Ian pulled her close, kissing her forehead softly, then sighed dramatically.

"For you, I can move mountains, my love."

Doctor Richard—not Dick—Schmidt changed that night. Weak minded as he was, Ian found it easy to alter his memories and even improve a bit on his personality. Not long after, Richard traded in the land yacht he drove for a more economic, less ostentatious model and started doing charity work. He even donated some of his time and skill to Doctors Without Borders and set off on a voyage of self-discovery to the Third World.

Of course Ian made sure he was kept under observation by one of his enforcer brethren. Richard Schmidt didn't know it, and would likely never remember what had brought it about, but he would be closely watched for the remainder of his days.

Ian also made arrangements for an evening wedding at a beautiful, old Catholic church in town. He'd sworn an oath to God all those years ago as a Crusader and he'd never gone back on his word. Jena was also Catholic and wanted all the trimmings for her wedding, including the beautiful old church where her mother could walk her down the aisle and tear up as her baby got married.

Ian was pleasantly surprised by his mate's mother, Lilian. Forty-seven she might be, but she was a beautiful woman in the prime of life. She welcomed Ian with suspicion at first, but once she saw how happy her daughter was with him, she warmed right up.

Julian was with her, of course. The charming enforcer had inserted himself into Lillian's life and looked like he was there to stay. Surprisingly, he hadn't told Lillian everything yet, but rather, had used his surprisingly strong abilities at mental persuasion to gain the woman's compliance.

Eventually she would have to be told about her heritage, but she was very healthy for one of the demi-vampir and Jena wanted to wait until after the wedding to break the startling news. Ian agreed. One thing at a time was enough to spring on the poor woman. Let her get used to him first, then he'd shatter her illusions of reality and explain how the world really worked.

Or perhaps he'd ask Julian or another of his old friends do it. Jena's mother was a looker, after all, and though she thought she was old in mortal terms, measuring by the lifespan of the average vampire, she was just a babe in the woods. Born demi-vampir, she should be given the choice to convert fully to the immortality she—or her ancestors, at least—should have had as her birthright.

Ian would take it up with Marc, but it could wait until after the wedding. And the honeymoon. Lillian's life wasn't in imminent danger from her demi-vampir condition, so they had time. Nothing was more important now, than joining his mate's life to his in the eyes of God.

When Ian first caught sight of his bride, framed in the dark doorway of the old church, his heart skipped a beat. She was so lovely.

The music started and she walked slowly down the aisle to him. The church was crowded with their friends, but he saw only her. When at last she stood beside him, he took her little hand in his. Her fingers were surprisingly cold with nerves.

I love you, you know. He sent his thoughts on waves of reassurance.

I love you back. Forever, Ian. She paused. *I mean that. I want forever with you.*

Do you mean—?

Yes. I want you to make me like you, but it'll have to wait until after the baby is born.

Baby? Ian felt faint. The implications were staggering.

Jena was still very much mortal. Any baby they had now would be demi-vampir, like her. Able to walk in the sun.

Stay with me, Papa. First we have to get hitched. No baby of ours will be born out of wedlock.

Ian felt tears gather behind his eyes, though he refused to let them fall. His woman was amazing. She brought him laughter and love, light and now...a baby.

While he would have preferred to wait until after she'd become immortal, God apparently had other plans. Ian would not argue with God, or Fate, or whatever had caused this miraculous moment to happen. All he knew was that he'd found the ultimate happiness in this realm and he would hold on to it—to her—for all he was worth.

Epilogue

By the next year on February fourteenth, Jena and Ian had fragile, baby, demi-vampir twins to look after. Leaving them with Christy and Sebastian for the night, Ian took Jena to the same little bistro where he'd spied on her with her date the year before.

"Nothing like coming full circle," he mused as he poured the wine. Jena was still demi-vampir and mortal. They'd decided that barring some unforeseen circumstance, Jena would stay mortal until the babies were a bit older. They weren't quite sure how becoming immortal would affect Jena's unique body chemistry, so they didn't want to take the chance of her not being able to be there during the day while the babies still needed her.

Ian was able to spend some time in the very early morning sun, but did even better in the late afternoon and twilight. With Jena's magic demi-vampir blood and multiple orgasms sustaining him, he fed only from her and was stronger than he'd ever been before.

"I liked it when you were watching over me, Ian. Though at first I found it a bit annoying." She toasted him with her wine. "You grew on me."

"Like a fungus, huh?"

She chuckled and tucked into the light meal she'd ordered while he just stared across at his good fortune. He still sometimes found it hard to believe this miracle had come to him. She was his salvation, his *raison d'être*. He didn't know how he'd existed for so long without her and couldn't envision a time when he could live without her. She was necessary to him now, in so many ways. Without her, he would cease to exist.

"Actually, I came to enjoy you glowering at me from the shrubbery and I missed you when you weren't there. Last Valentine's night, for example, when I went out to my car to meet Dick Schmidt," he growled at the mention of the other man's name, "you weren't there. I never told you, I nearly panicked, thinking something happened to you. It worried me when you suddenly weren't there."

Ian reached across the small table, much as Dick had done the year before, but with much more successful results. She turned her palm into his, smiling warmly up at him.

"I'll be with you always now, my love. For eternity."

About the Author

To learn more about Bianca D'Arc, please visit www.biancadarc.com. Send an email to Bianca at Bianca@biancadarc.com or join her Yahoo! group to join in the fun with other readers as well as Bianca D'Arc! http://groups.yahoo.com/group/BiancaDArc/

Overheard

Maya Banks

Dedication

To Jess for heading up such a fun project.

To Bianca and Gwen. Ganging up on Jess is awfully fun. We should do it again sometime.

Chapter One

The sun shone high overheard. The sky blazed brilliant blue, and not a single cloud marred the canvas. Sixty-five degrees on the first of February. It was what Gracie Evans loved most about living in south Texas. By the middle of the week, another cold front was poised to move through, dropping temps into the forties. Oh the horror.

Gracie stretched in her lawn chair and watched lazily as Jeremy Miller tended the barbeque while his wife, Gracie's best friend Michelle, hovered nearby.

"Come on, Gracie, get up and play," Wes Hoffman hollered from the yard.

She looked over to see him and Luke Forsythe tossing a football back and forth. Boneheads. She was more than comfortable right where she was. After a long week at work and not sleeping worth a damn last night, sitting up to eat was about as energetic as she planned to get.

Luke flopped onto the chair next to her. "What's up, Gracie? You're not usually such a stick-in-the-mud."

She shot him a dirty look. "Busy week at work. I'm just tired."

Of course, the worst part of the week had been last night. Her date with her current boyfriend had ended with the usual boring, obligatory sex, and quite frankly, she was tired of being disappointed in that area. She'd stayed up most of the night mustering the courage to call him this morning and break things off.

He hadn't taken it well.

"Earth to Gracie."

She blinked and looked back at Luke. "Sorry," she mumbled. "Lot on my mind."

Luke gave her a curious stare but seemed to sense she wasn't in the mood to talk. He got up and ambled over to talk to Jeremy. Wes joined them on the patio, a beer in hand.

Gracie let her gaze flit appreciatively over the men. Not bad considering they were her best friends and all. She wouldn't mind finding someone like Luke or Wes. Problem was she usually ended up with the frogs. Ugh.

Michelle eased into the chair next to Gracie, and Gracie looked over with a smile. "How you feeling, girlfriend?"

Michelle returned her smile. "Good. Tired but good."

Gracie eyed Michelle's cute little pregnancy pooch with a little jealousy. Jeremy was over the moon in love with his wife, and Gracie wondered what it felt like to have that sort of devotion. From what Michelle said, Jeremy was also dynamite in bed. Really, what more could you ask for in a man? Undying love and the know-how in the sack.

Gracie shook her head. She was really going to have to up her standards when it came to boyfriends. Boyfriend. Maybe that was her problem. She didn't need a boy. She wanted a man. Someone who could take her fantasies and make them reality.

"You sure are quiet today, Gracie."

Gracie grimaced. "Sorry. I broke up with Keith this morning."

Michelle jerked around in the lawn chair and all but pounced on Gracie. “Gracie, you didn’t!”

“Shhh,” Gracie hissed, looking up to see if the guys had heard. They already gave her a hard time about the men she chose to go out with. They’d be gleeful that her current relationship hadn’t worked out. The “I told you so’s” were already ringing in her ears.

“What happened?” Michelle whispered.

“I’ll talk to you about it later,” Gracie said, looking pointedly at the guys.

Michelle huffed but she didn’t protest further.

The two women lounged in the chairs while the men puttered around the grill. Gracie loved these times with the people she considered her best friends.

They got together pretty much every weekend. During hunting season, they spent weekends at the camp and hunted the mornings and evenings. When the weather was warm, they spent all their time at the beach, fishing and soaking up the sun. Gracie loved their group. She felt free to be herself.

Jeremy and Michelle had been married a year and they hosted most of the get togethers. Jeremy and Wes were both local cops, while Luke was a building contractor.

Wes was handsome in a carefree “I don’t give a shit” kind of way. He had blondish brown hair, and in the summer, it was liberally streaked with lighter shades. His sense of humor was what Gracie loved the most about him, that and he didn’t tend to get his underwear in a bunch at the least provocation. A more laid-back guy you wouldn’t find.

Luke, yeah, he was good looking. Blue eyes, light brown hair, and abs you could bounce a nickel off. But he was also a pain in the ass. A mouth-wateringly gorgeous pain in the ass, but an irritant nonetheless. His and Gracie’s relationship was a study in competition. Neither could stand to lose, and neither would ever back down from a dare.

Every year the outhunt and outfish contest usually boiled down to Luke and Gracie. Last year, Gracie had crowed when she'd bagged the biggest buck any of the group had ever killed. Luke had sworn to one-up her the following season.

But still, she wouldn't trade him for anything. The group worked well together. They were extremely loyal, and more importantly, they were always there for one another. Which was why she didn't want the guys to know she'd broken up with Keith. They'd make a huge deal out of it, and she simply wanted to forget the whole thing.

A shadow fell over her chair, and she looked up to see Wes standing over her with a beer in hand. He pressed the cold bottle to her arm, and she yelped and flinched.

He laughed. "Thought you might want a beer, Gracie."

"Gee, thanks."

He handed the beer to her then winked and ambled off again.

"Lug nut," she grumbled.

Michelle laughed. "You know you love him. He's cute when he's not being a pain in the ass."

Gracie nodded. "Yep, the two days of the year he's not a royal pain, he is downright cute."

"I heard that!" Wes called from the grill.

"You were supposed to," Gracie returned sweetly.

"I'm about ready to dish it up," Jeremy said. "Michelle, if you want to set the table, I'll have it up in about fifteen minutes."

"I'll help," Gracie said as she heaved herself out of her chair.

Luke turned his head and watched Gracie follow Michelle into the house. Her auburn curls jiggled down her back as she walked. He'd always loved her hair. It fit her carefree personality perfectly. Only she didn't seem so carefree today. He wondered what was bothering her. It wasn't like her to be quiet and withdrawn. And he didn't buy that line about a busy week at work. Gracie could do her job in her sleep.

"Do me a favor and take this in to Michelle," Jeremy said, ramming a tray into his gut.

Luke looked down to see a platter of sausage.

"Tell her the rest will be ten minutes."

Luke grunted. "Sure."

Luke walked toward the sliding door of the patio and eased inside. He strode through the living room and toward the kitchen. When he reached the doorway, Gracie's voice stopped him.

"I called him this morning and broke up with him."

Luke backed away and stood to the side. She'd broken up with Keith? Somehow that didn't surprise him. The guy was a complete pussy. No way he could keep pace with someone of Gracie's caliber.

He strained to hear the rest of the conversation.

"You called him the morning after you had sex and dumped him?" Michelle asked in disbelief.

"Yeah," Gracie replied.

Whoa. Harsh. Luke couldn't wait to hear why.

"Good God, girl. That must have been crushing to his ego," Michelle continued.

Luke nodded his agreement.

He heard Gracie sigh. "I don't care, Michelle. I'm tired of hooking up with guys who suck in bed. And I don't mean my tits either."

Michelle dissolved into laugher and Luke's eyebrows shot up.

"Was he that bad?" Michelle asked.

"He wasn't good," Gracie muttered. She sighed again. "Damn it, Chelle. I want something..."

Luke nearly hurt himself trying to press his ear closer to the doorway. What did Gracie want? This had to be good.

"I want someone who lights my fires. Who makes me think of nothing but taking every stitch of clothing off him and licking him from head to toe."

Luke shifted, an uncomfortable surge of heat racing to his crotch. Damn if the woman wasn't direct. He liked that in a girl. Didn't like stupid games and fluttering eyelashes.

"That's the problem with you, Gracie. You always settle for men who can't stand up to you," Michelle interjected.

Luke nodded in agreement. Michelle was right on there.

Another sigh from Gracie. "I want someone who can make my fantasies come alive, Chelle. Is that too much to ask? A guy who can be adventurous in bed and not come across like a freaking fruit loop?"

Fantasies? Luke shifted again and rubbed his palm across his shirt. Gracie had fantasies? Who knew?

"What kind of adventures are we talking about here, Gracie?" Michelle asked in a cautious voice.

Yeah, what kind of fantasies? Damn it, he only had a few minutes before Jeremy was going to come busting in with the rest of the food. Then he'd never find out what made Gracie tick.

There was a long, silent pause.

"Nothing illegal," Gracie cracked. "At least I don't think they are."

"Quit joking and spill it," Michelle said. "The guys will be in soon."

"Oh, I fantasize about bondage, a little spanking, maybe a whip or two. The idea of being tied up gets me hotter than I'd like to admit," Gracie said ruefully. "But..."

But what? Luke wanted to yell.

"More than anything I'd love to experience a ménage."

"Gracie!" Michelle exclaimed. "Really?"

"Yeah," Gracie said in a low voice. "Two sexy men, all their attention on me, pleasuring me? Yeah, I think about it a lot. I just don't know how to make it happen."

"Holy shit," Michelle whispered loudly. "Have you thought about taking out an adult ad or something?"

"Yeah, I have," Gracie replied. "I've thought about it a lot. But the thought scares me. Who knows what kind of freaks are out there."

Adult ad? Luke wanted to march in and throttle her. He would have but he was still thrown for a loop by what she'd admitted. Gracie, *his* Gracie, had triple X fantasies.

"Face it, Chelle. I'm not sure there's a man out there who can satisfy my needs in bed. Maybe I'm expecting too much. I just know I'm not settling for less ever again. I'm done with the Keiths of this world. If I can't find a man, I'll stick to my toys and self-gratification."

Not sure there's a man out there who could satisfy her huh. Luke's mind whirled with all he'd overheard. So she wanted a threesome. It was obvious Luke had spent far too much time looking at Gracie as a best buddy and a hunting/fishing partner. It certainly wasn't every day he found a woman who wanted all the things that had gotten him tossed out of so many women's beds.

Ménage. She wanted a ménage. He couldn't wait to talk to Wes. He had a feeling his buddy would be very interested in what their good pal Gracie wanted out of her sex life.

Man enough? She didn't realize it yet, but she'd thrown down the challenge. And damn if he wasn't going to be the man to answer it.

Chapter Two

Gracie dug into her food, sighing with pleasure as the tender meat hit her tongue.

"Good?" Jeremy asked.

"Run away with me," Gracie declared. "What does Chelle have that I don't? We can live on your barbeque and be beach bums."

Jeremy grinned and started to reply.

Gracie held up a hand. "No, don't answer that. I'm not up for a list of the ways I don't measure up."

Wes and Jeremy looked curiously at her while Luke made it a point to stare down at his plate. Gracie cringed. Instead of coming out jokingly as she'd intended, it sounded sad and resigned.

She glanced over at Michelle and made an "oops" face the others couldn't see. Then she focused back on her food, cutting another bite of the brisket.

Her breakup with Keith bothered her more than she liked. Not only had the sex been a disaster, but his reaction to the surprise she'd planned still made her cringe in embarrassment. He'd made her feel like a freak. Not what a woman wanted to feel like when she was trying to be wild and sexy.

Weren't men supposed to like that sort of thing? Didn't they all complain because women weren't adventurous enough in bed? Ha! She'd yet to find a man who liked sex with the frequency and imagination she did.

Maybe she *was* a freak.

She cleared her throat and looked over at Luke. "How's Ellie doing? I haven't seen her much since the wedding. Jake seems awfully protective of her."

"He has a reason to be," Luke said with a grimace. "But she's doing good. They seem happy."

"Isn't she going to counseling?" Michelle interjected.

Luke nodded. "Yeah, that whole thing with Ray really fucked her up."

"Stupid son of a bitch," Wes muttered. "I don't trust that little breakdown he had on public television. Seems too calculating to me."

Jeremy raised his brow. "You think he'll try something?"

"Not unless he has a death wish," Luke said. "Jake will kill him if he comes near Ellie again."

"And I won't exactly be knocking myself out to stop him," Wes said.

Gracie shook her head. "Ellie's a sweet girl. I hate that she's been through so much. But Jake's good for her."

"He'd be good for me, too," Michelle broke in, a devilish glint to her eye.

"Hey," Jeremy protested as he reached over to tweak Michelle's arm.

Gracie laughed. God, she loved these guys. She could never stay down in the dumps for long around them. "If Chelle doesn't want you, Jeremy, you're welcome at my house."

"Are you propositioning my husband?" Michelle demanded.

Jeremy rubbed a hand over his chin. “I kind of like being fought over.”

“Cat fights are sexy,” Wes said with a snicker.

Gracie rolled her eyes. “Like any girl has a chance with Jeremy. He’s so gaga over Michelle, it’s nauseating.”

“Just like I like him,” Michelle said with a smug grin.

Michelle stood and began clearing the table. Gracie got up to help and started collecting the plates. As Michelle began running water in the sink, she looked out the kitchen window and tensed.

“Uh oh, Gracie.”

Gracie didn’t like the sound of that uh oh.

Jeremy evidently didn’t either. He went to stand behind his wife so he could look out.

Michelle turned around to Gracie. “Keith just pulled up.”

“Oh great,” Gracie muttered as she plunked down the plates she was holding.

“Trouble, Gracie?” Wes asked in a concerned voice.

She flashed him a reassuring smile. “Nothing I can’t handle.” She walked toward the door, determined to meet Keith outside rather than take the inevitable confrontation inside. “Y’all excuse me for a second. This shouldn’t take long.”

Luke followed her with his gaze until she left the house with a bang. Wes looked over at him questioningly, but Luke played dumb. He didn’t want to let on that he’d overheard Gracie’s conversation with Michelle.

“What’s going on with those two?” Jeremy asked Michelle as they continued to stare out the window.

“She broke up with him this morning,” Michelle murmured.

Wes got up from the table, carrying the plates Gracie had left. He walked to the sink and set them down before peering out the window himself. Luke was dying to do the same, but he made himself sit and appear only mildly interested.

“Can’t say it surprises me,” Wes said with a shrug as he returned to sit at the table. “She needs a man she can’t run over so easily.”

Luke looked at his friend in surprise. On that point they agreed, though they’d never discussed Gracie’s love life before. Hadn’t exactly been high on their priority lists.

“He looks angry,” Michelle said anxiously.

Both Wes and Luke shot to their feet and walked to the window to look out. They were all understandably wary after all that Ellie had endured at her ex-husband’s hands. No way would they stand by and let Gracie take the brunt of some punk’s anger. Keith did look pretty pissed and Gracie took a step backwards as they all watched.

“I’m going out there,” Luke muttered. “I want to make sure the dickhead doesn’t get carried away.”

“Jeremy and Wes are the cops, maybe they should go,” Michelle said, her frown deepening as she watched her friend.

“More reason for me to go,” Luke said. “I can get away with decking the asshole better than they can.”

He didn’t wait for a response. He strode for the door and quietly let himself out.

Neither Gracie nor Keith must have heard him because they never turned around. Luke eased down the steps into the yard. Their heated conversation filled his ears, and he stopped so he could listen from the distance.

“Damn it, Gracie, what was I supposed to do? You acted like some kind of a whore. I wasn’t expecting it.”

Gracie clenched her fists at her side.

"Just because I suggested we do something other than the usual suck your dick and missionary that makes me a whore?" she all but yelled.

"Be quiet for God's sake!"

"No, Keith, I won't be quiet. It's over. I don't know why you're here, but it sure as hell won't change my mind. I said all I had to say this morning."

"You're dumping me?" he asked incredulously. "Shit, Gracie, you're being unreasonable. You should have warned me or something. You had *nipple* rings of all things. Like some kind of cheap tramp. What on earth possessed you? Is that what you made me wait a month without sex for? So you could spring this weird ass surprise on me? And then you go on about how you want me to take control and for you not to have to decide how we do it all the time. Give a guy a break."

Nipple rings? Oh Jesus. Gracie had nipple rings. This most certainly was a new development. Luke had seen her in a bikini on many occasions, and he damn sure would have noticed nipple rings.

So Gracie was trying to branch out and the pussy boyfriend had thrown a fit. Well, good for her for dumping him. He obviously didn't deserve her.

"That's exactly what I'm doing," Gracie said coldly. "Giving you a break. We're done. Finito."

Anger flashed on Keith's face, and Luke started forward. He knew that look and it could only mean trouble.

"You teasing bitch," Keith snarled.

He made a grab for her arm, but Gracie sidestepped him and rammed her knee into his groin.

"Cock-sucking bastard!" she hissed as he fell to the ground.

Luke stepped between them and hauled Keith up by his shirt. The man was still pale with pain and clutching his privates for all he was worth.

Luke slammed him against Keith's truck and got in his face. "If I ever see you within ten feet of Gracie again, I'll make what she just did look like a blow job. You got me?"

Keith grunted and struggled to get loose. "Yeah, I get it. Get your fucking hands off me. You're welcome to the psycho bitch."

Luke decked him. Keith fell to the ground, blood spurting from his nose. Keith grabbed his face with both hands, howling in pain.

He scrambled to his feet and fumbled to open his truck door. "You son of a bitch! If you broke my nose, I'm pressing charges."

Luke chuckled and jerked his thumb in the direction of the kitchen window. "You do that, pussy boy. But you ought to know two cops are watching from that window over there, and I imagine they'll swear they didn't see any such thing."

Keith threw himself into the truck, swearing and swiping at the blood running down his face. In a few seconds, he spun out of the driveway, spewing a trail of rocks and dirt several feet high.

Luke turned back to Gracie who wore a look of astonishment on her face.

"You okay?" he asked gently.

"Yeah, I'm good." She looked up at him, her eyebrows arched in question. "What the hell was that all about?"

Luke knew why she was confused. He'd never intruded on her business like that. Gracie was more than able to take care of herself. It was something he admired about her.

He shrugged and put a hand on her shoulder. “Just looked like you could use the help, that’s all.”

“Yeah, well, thanks,” she mumbled as they started back toward the house.

As they stopped at the steps, she looked up at him, her bottom lip stuck between her teeth, a sure sign of agitation.

“You didn’t...you didn’t hear our conversation did you?” she asked nervously.

Luke almost smiled. Yeah, he supposed Gracie would about die if she knew he’d overheard that and more. From what he’d gleaned from her conversation with Michelle and then her fight with Keith, it looked like she was spreading her wings a bit and venturing into new territory. Territory he was intimately familiar with.

“Nah, I’d just come out when he made a move toward you,” he lied. “Looked like he was trying to hurt you.”

“Well, thanks,” she said again, her shoulders slumping in relief.

“No problem. What are friends for?”

He threw his arm around her neck, letting his hand dangle over her shoulder, something he’d done a million times before. Only now, he was very aware of the proximity of his hand to her breasts. And those nipple rings he was dying to see.

Chapter Three

"So you going to tell me what the hell went on out there?" Wes asked as he popped open another beer.

Luke flopped onto his couch and took a long swig of his own beer. He and Wes had left Jeremy's earlier and had ended up at Luke's place. Luke knew Wes was curious over his interference, not that Wes would have done things any differently if he'd been outside when Keith made his move at Gracie.

He took another fortifying gulp before he eased the bottle from his lips. "Let's just say it's been an interesting and informative day.

Wes leaned back in the arm chair and propped his feet up on Luke's coffee table. "How so?"

Luke shook his head. Where to start? With the easy part he guessed. "Keith was being an asshole. He was ripping on Gracie, and she told him to take a hike. He went after her and Gracie kneed him in the balls."

"Good for her," Wes said, performing a mock salute with his beer bottle.

"I broke his nose for good measure."

Wes looked at him and shook his head. "Shit, tell me I'm not going to have to arrest your ass when he presses charges."

Luke laughed. "He's a pussy. Besides, I told him you and Jeremy were watching and would swear you didn't see anything."

"Gee, thanks," Wes said dryly. "Just what I need, to be arrested with you."

Luke fiddled with his beer, tapping his finger in restless staccato against the cool glass. He hesitated to tell Wes what he'd overheard. Why, he couldn't say. They'd never exactly been discreet with each other, and he knew Wes would find it as surprising as he had. But something held him back.

"What's eating you?" Wes spoke up, intruding on Luke's thoughts. "You've been acting weird all afternoon. You said the day had been informative. So what's the news?"

Luke sighed and leaned forward to set his beer on the coffee table. "It's about Gracie."

Wes cocked an eyebrow. "What about her? You weren't really surprised she dumped her pussy boyfriend, were you?"

Luke shook his head. "I'm not talking about the wimp, and no, I'm not all together surprised she dumped him. Even less so after what I heard her talking to Michelle about."

"Ah hell, man, what were you doing eavesdropping on the girls? Gracie will kick your ass if she finds out."

Luke grinned. Yeah, she wouldn't hesitate to lay him out. He got the oddest tingle just thinking about her getting in his face. He shook his head. It was the nipple rings, it had to be. He couldn't get his mind off what her nipples must look like. Hell.

He cleared his throat. "She, uh, well, she said some interesting things."

Wes leaned forward, dropping his feet to the floor with a thud. "Now you've got me curious. What the hell did she say?"

“Apparently she dumped the pussy because he sucked in bed.”

“Yeah, well, again, that’s no surprise. She probably ate him alive,” Wes said.

Luke cocked his head sideways and stared at his friend. “Tell me something, Wes. Have you ever thought about having sex with Gracie?”

Wes choked on his beer and coughed several times in succession. “Sex? With Gracie? Shit man, no, not really. I mean she’s hot, don’t get me wrong. Seriously hot. But...”

“Seriously hot, huh. So you have thought about it, you lying sack of shit,” Luke said on a laugh.

“You have eyes, man. The girl is a walking goddess. What guy wouldn’t get a hard-on looking at her?”

“Well, get this,” Luke said, leaning toward Wes. “I overheard her telling Michelle that she was tired of men not satisfying her in bed. That she has fantasies she wants to live out.”

Wes sat up straighter, his attention focused on Luke. “What kind of fantasies?”

Luke shrugged casually, but his blood was racing just thinking about all she’d said. “Bondage, a little spanking...and she wants to take on two guys at the same time.”

“Whoa,” Wes said as he flopped back in his chair. “She said all that?”

“There’s more,” Luke continued on. “Apparently she wanted pussy boy to do a little experimenting in bed and he freaked. He called her a whore.”

“That little son of a bitch,” Wes growled. “I knew I should have gone outside with you.”

“She has nipple rings. Must be recent. Keith evidently didn’t receive the news so well judging by his comments.”

"Holy fucking shit. Nipple rings?"

"Yeah. Now tell me you aren't picturing Gracie in the buff with nipple rings dangling from those perfect breasts."

"Jesus."

"My thoughts exactly," Luke mumbled.

"She wants two guys? She said that?"

"Oh, hell yeah. She said that and a lot more. She wants a guy who isn't afraid to call the shots. Someone who will tie her up, spank her ass and fuck her brains out."

"Goddamn."

Luke laughed. "Is that all you can say?"

"I'm speechless," Wes said, his mouth still open in shock.

"Glad I'm not the only one all fucked up over it."

"Does she know you heard all that?"

"Hell no. She wouldn't speak to me for a year," Luke said.

Wes fell silent, his eyes thoughtful. Luke knew Wes's brain was spinning a mile a minute. He also knew Wes was rapidly coming to the same conclusion he had.

"Hell, if that's what she wants..."

"Yeah," Luke said. "Tell me you aren't thinking the same thing I am."

Wes grunted. "I'd have to be fucking gay not to react to something like that. I mean she's hot. I've always thought so."

Luke looked over at his friend. "Valentine's is just two weeks away. Should be enough time for you to make arrangements to be off work."

Wes's eyes narrowed. "What are you thinking about?"

Luke took in a deep breath then grinned. "Well, we've already established the fact that Gracie is hot. We're both attracted to her. Neither of us has any problem with nipple rings or bondage, and we have considerable experience in the threesome arena. So it seems to me that maybe we should give Gracie a Valentine's Day to remember."

"What if she won't go for it?" Wes asked. "I don't want to piss her off and I sure don't want to mess up my friendship with her. We have too much fun for that shit."

"She'll go for it," Luke said confidently.

He'd seen the longing in her eyes, the need for something she probably couldn't even explain. He knew it because he'd felt the same thing. He also knew that he was the man who could give it to her.

Wes scrubbed a hand over his closely shaved goatee in a thoughtful motion. "I don't know, man. It's not like we're going to fuck some chick we won't ever see again. This is Gracie we're talking about. What happens when it's over with? I don't want there to be any awkward shit."

"You're over thinking this," Luke said impatiently. "We give Gracie an experience she won't ever forget. We show her things she's been craving. If anything it makes us even closer. I mean there's no way in hell I'd fuck her and just go on like nothing ever happened. We both like her a hell of a lot. More than any other woman apart from Michelle, that's for sure. I don't see the problem here."

"Just how much do you like her?" Wes asked, a peculiar expression on his face.

Luke shifted uncomfortably. What the hell kind of question was that? "I—I care about her," he said lamely.

Wes continued to stare at him. "Do you have a thing for her?"

"Shut the fuck up," Luke growled. "Jesus, this is sex. Gracie's our friend. Our very gorgeous, hot friend. You can't tell me you wouldn't like to get next to her."

Wes took a sip of his beer. "No, I can't tell you that. But wanting something or knowing I'd enjoy it is different than actually doing it. Look, I just don't want to fuck things up between us all."

"What if she wanted it?" Luke challenged. "I mean what if she wanted what we could give her? Would you be so reluctant then?"

Wes thought for a minute then shook his head. "Hell no. I just don't want to hurt her. That's all I'm saying."

"Well, shit, Wes. Do you think I'd do anything to hurt her? She's one of my best friends. I want to make it good for her."

"You're serious about this."

"Fuck. No, I've just spent the last ten minutes going on about my plan to seduce Gracie for nothing."

"No need to be sarcastic," Wes said with a chuckle. "Okay, you've convinced me. This is your idea, so you plan it. Tell me when and where to show up. I'll be there. But if she shows any sign of not wanting this, I'm out."

Luke scowled at him. "No shit, dumbass. It's not my plan to rape her for God's sake. But I'm telling you, she wants something. Something she doesn't quite understand but knows she wants. You didn't hear the things she said or the *way* she said them. And I think I can give her what she wants."

Wes looked quietly at him, studying him with that cop look he was so famous for. "Yeah, maybe you can."

Chapter Four

Gracie twisted restlessly in her chair and flipped another contract in the to be signed pile. Mondays were always busy. Tickets to process, contracts to look over. It was dull, tedious work, but it paid the bills, and she could do it with half a brain. Important when the other half was consumed with her nonexistent sex life.

Yesterday's encounter with Keith had only reinforced that she'd made the right decision. She still felt the uncomfortable burn of embarrassment that Luke had stepped in when Keith had gone over the line. She didn't like Luke seeing yet another of her failures.

Her office door swung open, and she looked up to see Luke standing there. She blinked, wondering if she'd conjured him. She smiled welcomingly.

"Hey, what are you doing here?"

He ambled further into her office, his thumbs thrust into his jeans pockets. Jeans that were tightly molded to his muscular legs. His leather jacket hung loosely to his waist, and underneath she could see he wore a simple T-shirt. Obviously a day he wasn't meeting prospective clients.

"Hey, Gracie," he said, returning her smile. "I was in the neighborhood and wondered if you wanted to grab lunch with me."

Her smile widened. "Barbeque?"

He chuckled. "As if I'd suggest anything else."

She made a grab for her jacket on the floor at her feet before standing. "As long as you're buying."

As she rounded the desk, his arm came out, and he pressed his hand to the small of her back to usher her out the door. It was an intimate gesture, one that puzzled her. He was usually all about punching her in the arm or pointing out a nonexistent spot on her shirt so she'd look down and he could chuck her nose.

They walked outside, and Gracie shivered slightly. Damn cold front had moved in overnight. The sky was overcast and gray, and a cold drizzle escaped in fine droplets.

She slid into Luke's truck and sank into the heated leather seats with a contented sigh. She'd given him hell when he'd bought the truck. Top of the line, tricked out, no expense spared. He spent money like it was nothing. But then he did have a lot of it to burn.

"Cold?" Luke asked as he started the engine and turned the heat on full blast.

She grumbled under her breath and stuck her hands out to the vents. He knew damn well she was freezing her ass off. Anything below fifty degrees and she was breaking out the winter parka.

They drove a few miles to the Barbeque Shack and pulled into the crowded parking lot. Aside from a Mexican restaurant and a hole-in-the-wall burger joint, this was the only other place to eat without driving into the neighboring town. Which was fine with Gracie, because if it wasn't grilled and slathered with barbeque sauce, it wasn't worth eating.

Luke walked ahead of her treating her to a look at those very tight jeans stretched across a very nice ass. His hair was all messed up as usual, but that was Luke. The wind blew at it, ruffling it up and sending it scattering across his head. She nearly reached up to smooth it, but caught herself before she did.

He held the door open for her, and she walked by him, sniffing appreciatively as the mixture of leather and the smell that was Luke sifted through her nostrils.

Minutes later, they were sitting at a table by the window sipping their drinks and waiting for their order to come. Luke leaned back in his chair and gazed lazily at her.

"Tell me something, Gracie. How come you and I haven't ever gone out?"

She nearly choked on her drink. She set it down with a plunk and wheezed as she tried to make the last swallow go down.

"What?" she gasped.

His eyes narrowed. "You heard me."

"Well hell, Luke, I don't know what to say."

Her mind reeled as she stared at him. What on earth had possessed him?

"We like each other, right?"

"Well, of course," she said crossly. She wasn't sure she liked where this conversation was heading. Now was not the time for Luke to get some strange bug up his ass.

She was feeling oddly vulnerable after her latest dead-end relationship. Like she was some freak of nature, destined to never find a guy who understood her, much less one who could satisfy her.

"We get along great. We understand each other," Luke continued.

Yeah, right. If he only knew. He understood she was a nice girl who kept picking the wrong guy. He had no idea that underneath all the sweetness was a woman itching to break out. She was tired of being good. The girl next door. She wanted to be bad. And she was damn sure tired of being viewed as little sister, good pal, hunting and fishing partner.

"Is there a point to all this?" she asked.

"Yeah," he said slowly. "There is. I'm trying to figure out why we've never gone out on a date."

She stared at him for a long second, debating whether to even go there. But she wasn't a liar, and she wasn't big on playing games. So she just told the truth.

"Because you never asked," she said softly.

They were interrupted by the waitress bringing their plates and dumping them in front of them. Gracie was grateful for the break because Luke was looking at her like he could crawl right under her skin and see everything she was hiding.

The waitress took her sweet time in leaving, and as she started away, she slid a napkin across the table toward Luke. Gracie didn't give it a single thought until Luke picked it up and looked over his shoulder, a look of surprise on his face.

"What's wrong?" Gracie asked, finally breaking the silence between them.

Luke turned back around, shaking his head. "She gave me her phone number. Wrote it on the napkin."

A surge of irritation rippled through her chest. "That's probably one reason we've never gone out," she muttered.

"But you were sitting right there," he said, ignoring her comment. "How the hell did she know we weren't here together, that you aren't my girlfriend or something?"

Gracie burst out laughing. "Luke, are you feeling well today? I swear you aren't yourself. Half the town is used to seeing us together. No one's ever assumed you were interested in me."

"Well, what do they know?" he growled.

He stared across the table at her, his blue eyes sparking with something she wasn't used to seeing. At least not when he was looking at her.

"I'm asking now, Gracie."

She looked dumbly at him. "You want us to go out? As in a real date? I mean because we usually hook up on the weekends anyway."

He dropped the napkin and leaned forward impatiently. "I mean you and me on a date. No Jeremy, Michelle or Wes. Friday night."

She blinked in surprise. A peculiar sensation ran circles in her belly. She felt *nervous*. For God's sake. This was Luke.

A real date. She sank back in her chair, still staring at him like he'd lost his mind.

"Well?"

"Uh...okay. I mean if you really want to. Friday night is okay."

He smiled then, relaxing back into his seat. His blue eyes held a warm glow, a *triumphant* warm glow.

"All right then. I'll pick you up around five. We'll go into Beaumont to eat."

She nodded, suddenly unable to taste the food she'd stuffed into her mouth. A date. With Luke Forsythe. Her best friend Luke Forsythe. Holy hell. Michelle was going to shit a brick when she heard this.

A mental groan echoed in her head. They'd never hear the end of it from Wes and Jeremy.

"He did what?"

Gracie winced as Michelle nearly shrieked her ear off.

"Holy cow, Gracie, you and Luke?"

"Yeah, I know," Gracie mumbled as she put the phone back to her ear. Hopefully Michelle's scream fest was over. "Do me a favor. Don't tell Jeremy about this. Or Wes."

"Well, of course I'm going to tell Jeremy. I tell him everything."

I tell him everything, Gracie silently mimicked. Hell.

"And then Jeremy will tell Wes, because he tells Wes everything. And then Wes will tell everyone because that's what he does," Gracie gritted out.

"Gracie, hon, I hate to tell you this, but within five minutes of you and Luke being seen out on a Friday night when everyone and their mama knows you both always come over here, everyone's going to know anyway."

"Fuck me," Gracie muttered. "I don't know why the hell I agreed to this. He's got to be out of his damn mind."

"Why, because he asked you out? I'd say that's the first smart thing he's done in a long time," Michelle said loyally.

"I just hope it doesn't screw things up for everyone," Gracie hedged. "We've got a good thing. No need for Luke and me to fuck it up."

"Oh, please. We're big kids, Gracie. We can handle a little tension without freaking out and going our separate ways. Stop looking for reasons not to go out with him and just do it. You've got to admit he is one sexy beast."

"You are so not helping here," Gracie grumbled.

Michelle laughed. "Go. Enjoy yourself. You said yourself, you were tired of being with men who can't satisfy you. I can't imagine Luke disappointing a woman in bed. Not with his considerable equipment."

"Michelle!" Grace's admonishment nearly strangled her. "What the hell do you know about his equipment?"

"Oh, you are one lying bitch if you tell me you weren't looking every bit as hard as I was when the men went skinny dipping two summers ago. That was before Jeremy and I got married, and I was staring every chance I got."

There was a long silence then Michelle burst into laughter. "You were watching. Admit it, Gracie."

"All right, all right, so I was watching. Hard not to when they were flopping around in the buff."

"Uh huh. Now tell me you didn't get an eyeful of his equipment."

Gracie felt heat rush to her cheeks. She hadn't thought about that time in a long while. But yeah, she remembered. She'd stared in pure feminine appreciation at the hard bodies and the gorgeous cocks. Watched while they got out and as the water ran down their bodies. Oh yeah, she'd looked. And looked. And lamented that she'd never had one that nice.

A ripple of awareness skittered over her body. Her nipples hardened, and the rings twitched in response.

"Yeah, I got an eyeful."

There was a long pause before Michelle said, "This is a good thing, Gracie. Maybe...maybe Luke is exactly what you need."

Gracie licked her lips and felt nervous jitters tickle her stomach. Maybe Michelle was right. After all, no man in her past could ever stack up next to Luke. Luke, well, he was in a class all by himself. So why wasn't she looking forward to their date?

"Yeah, maybe," Gracie mumbled. "Look, Chelle, I gotta run. It's getting late, and I've got a ton of shit to do at the office tomorrow."

They rang off, and Gracie sat there for a long time, thinking about her lunch with Luke. She felt edgy, unsatisfied. Horny as hell. Had Luke done that to her? Had the idea of going out with him in the capacity of something other than a buddy got her all hot and bothered?

She felt a date with BOB coming on. And later, as she relaxed after a BOB-induced orgasm, she was irritated to note that she'd fantasized about Luke the entire time she'd gotten herself off. And his damn equipment.

Chapter Five

Gracie waited nervously for Luke to arrive at her house. She'd dressed meticulously, changing her mind a thousand times, and it pissed her off to no end. She, who never spent more than five minutes on dress, hair and makeup, had spent well over an hour angsting over every aspect.

If that didn't make her pathetic, she didn't know what else would.

She looked down one more time at the black sweater she'd chosen. She looked good in black. It went well with her auburn hair. And if she'd squeezed herself into a pair of jeans she hadn't been able to wear in several months, it certainly wasn't because she wanted to look hot for Luke. She just didn't want to look like a fat ass.

She blew a curl out of her face for the hundredth time and wished she'd used more hairspray. But then if they went anywhere with candles or little kerosene lamps on the tables, she'd go up in flames with as much shit as she had in her hair.

Finally, she heard Luke's truck and headed for the door. She met him halfway across the lawn, and he looked at her in surprise.

"I would have come and gotten you, Gracie."

She shrugged. "I'm here."

He took a minute to look her over. "You look nice."

She smiled at him and willed herself not to shake. "Thanks."

He guided her back toward the truck and opened her door for her. He got in on his side and turned up the heat before backing out of her driveway.

She studied him as he maneuvered. He must have gone home and shaved because he usually wore a shadow by now. He wore a short-sleeved polo shirt that stretched tightly across his biceps. He worked out regularly with Wes, Jeremy and Jake, something they'd started a year and half back, and the results were downright yummy. She couldn't wait for the summer when they'd run around shirtless. She hadn't seen Luke's six pack since last summer, and it had looked pretty damn good then.

"How does seafood sound?" he asked as he looked over at her.

"Sounds great to me."

They lapsed into silence, and Gracie wondered if she were the only one who felt the awkwardness between them. If they were going over to Michelle's, they'd be chatting it up, talking about the work week and the weekend ahead. But they were on a date. And that changed everything.

She let out a small sigh and slouched down in her seat. To her surprise, Luke reached over and slid his hand over hers. He tucked his fingers against her palm and ran his thumb over the back of her hand.

"Relax, Gracie. We can do this."

"But *why* are we doing this?" she blurted out.

It just seemed so stupid to ruin the easy-going rapport between them. She snuck another glance at him to see him smiling. What the hell was so funny?

He left his hand over hers as they drove into town. When they reached the restaurant, he hopped out of the truck and hurried around to open her door. He reached up to help her down, and she landed close to him. Close enough to smell his cologne and to feel his body heat.

He tucked a curl behind her ear, his fingers glancing over her cheek. "You look beautiful."

Her face grew warm. Before she could respond, he wrapped an arm around her shoulders and guided her toward the entrance. A couple. They were acting just like a couple, and it was weirding her out.

Once inside, Luke ordered fish and she ordered shrimp. They both ordered a beer and sat back to wait on the food.

"So how are we doing so far?" Luke asked as he watched her across the table.

"I don't know, Luke. I feel like this is a test or something, only I don't know the rules or what we're supposed to be doing."

He leaned forward and stared intently at her, his blue eyes glowing in the dim light. "You're a gorgeous woman, Gracie. Why do you find it so hard to believe that I'd want to go out with you?"

Her eyebrows furrowed. "Maybe because we've been friends for years and you've never even hinted at it before now?"

He shrugged. "I wasn't ready."

"And you are now?"

"Maybe."

He took a long swallow of his beer and arched one brow at her. "If you're so unconvinced then why did you agree to go out with me? What is it you want from this?"

Busted. He'd turned the tables on her completely. She licked her lips and thought about what to say.

"I don't know," she finally said. "Something about it intrigued me. Maybe a part of me lit up at the idea. I'm confused."

"That's what I love so much about you, Gracie," Luke said.

She laughed. "What, that I'm a confused numb nut?"

"No, that you're honest. You're direct. There's no pretense about you. It's sexy as hell."

She blinked in surprise. She hadn't exactly expected him to say that.

The waitress delivered their food and Gracie dug in, glad to have a distraction from the current conversation. Luke was attracted to her, and she was damn well attracted to him, but it wasn't as easy as going home and having sex. This was Luke. One of her best friends on earth. His respect meant a lot to her. So did his friendship. She didn't want to do anything to fuck up either one.

If they had sex and things didn't work out, how would it affect them? Could they really pick up and go on like it hadn't happened? Continue to spend as much time together as they did? Go hunting and fishing and hang out at Jeremy and Michelle's?

"You're putting way too much thought into this," Luke said mildly.

She looked up guiltily to see him watching her. "I'm sorry. I'm doing my best to ruin the evening before it even starts."

"Just relax. We always have a good time together."

She smiled. "Yeah, we do."

"Eat up. We'll take a drive. Go out by the lake and watch the stars."

"That sounds great," she said.

♥♥♥

The moon was rising when they pulled up and parked at the overlook.

"Want to get out?" Luke asked as he cut the engine.

"And freeze to death?" Gracie asked in mock horror.

"I'll keep you warm."

She stared at him, shivering slightly at his promise. Well, she was no wimp, and she was willing to see where this took them. She opened the door and stepped into the crisp night air.

She breathed in deep and stared out over the water. It was a crystal clear night and the stars shone brightly in the sky.

Luke walked around the front of the truck and leaned against the hood. She moved to stand beside him. Damn it, she was already cold. No way she was going to stand out here for long.

He reached for her, curling an arm around her and pulling her to stand in front of him. Then he wrapped both arms around her body until her back was firmly melded to his chest. He tucked her head underneath his chin.

"Better?" he asked.

She was warm from head to toe. There wasn't an inch of her skin that didn't feel like someone had taken a blowtorch to it. She nodded her head.

"So tell me something about you I don't already know," he said against her hair.

She laughed. "But you already know everything about me."

"Not true. I think there's quite a bit I don't know about you," he said softly. "I want to know what makes you tick, Gracie. What your dreams are. Your fantasies."

"My fantasies?" she squeaked.

She closed her eyes. No way was she going there. She'd tried that with Keith and it had led to their immediate breakup.

"Hmmm, I can feel you blushing. You must have some juicy fantasies."

She stiffened in his arms. She didn't want to waste her time or his. No, she didn't really want to go into it, but if he were going to scare off, she'd rather it be now than later. If he couldn't handle hearing about the real Gracie, then he certainly wasn't worth her time.

Luke felt the rioting emotions in her. Knew she was waging a battle with herself over whether to share that part of herself with him. He held his breath, hoping she'd trust him.

She turned in his arms, the light of battle in her eyes. She looked at him almost defiantly. "I'll tell you mine but you have to tell me yours."

She was testing him. He could tell. She thought he'd tuck tail and run just like her last pussy boyfriend. She was afraid to share that intimate part for fear of rejection, and who could blame her with the way dipshit had responded.

"Oh, I'll tell you mine," he said calmly.

"I like sex," she blurted. "Good sex. Or I should say I'd love good sex."

Luke raised an eyebrow. "Boyfriends not satisfying you in that department?"

She ducked her head. "No," she mumbled.

"Go on," he urged.

She stepped back a bit and took a deep breath. "I want a man who doesn't feel like he has to stop and ask permission every step of the way. I want someone who can take control and make it good for both of us. I want someone who is creative and doesn't have to be coached."

"You don't want someone who has to be told how to satisfy you," Luke spoke up.

"Exactly! And...and...I want to experiment, do something different, and I'd love to have a partner who could make that happen without making me feel like a freak."

They were getting somewhere now.

"What would you like to do, Gracie?" he prompted.

She wrinkled her nose and grinned. "I have a kinky streak in me a mile wide. I'd love to be tied up, spanked and my brains fucked out. And...I'd really love to have a threesome."

"Another woman?" Luke asked, pretending ignorance.

She shook her head adamantly. "No, me and two men."

"Ahh."

"What's that supposed to mean?" she asked defensively.

He put his hands out to her shoulders. "Gracie, it doesn't mean anything. You're not a freak. Lots of women have these fantasies. They're healthy, normal fantasies."

She relaxed a little. "You don't think I'm weird?"

He chuckled. "Yeah, I think you're weird, but not because you have kinky sex fantasies."

She surprised him by throwing her arms around him and hugging tight. He eased his arms around her and held her, running a hand through her curls. He probably shouldn't push things yet, but he'd been dying to taste her all night.

He tugged gently at her hair until her head fell back. He cupped a hand to her cheek and gently ran his thumb down her jaw. Her lips fell open in silent invitation and it was all he needed.

His lips found hers, hot, flushed and needy. She tasted sweet, and she felt incredibly soft against his hard body. He loved that, loved the way she fit so perfectly against him.

Her mouth opened wider against his kiss and the tip of her tongue feathered over his. He caught it and sucked it further into his mouth. Their tongues rolled and tangled as the sounds of their breathing echoed into the night.

If they were anywhere but at the lake on a cold night, Luke would lay her down and strip her naked. He'd get between her thighs and slide so deep into her pussy that she wouldn't know where he began and she ended.

With more willpower than he thought he possessed, he pulled away from her.

"Wow," she whispered.

"Yeah, wow," he agreed. "I had a feeling we'd be like an inferno if we ever got together."

She stuck her hands in her pockets and looked away for a minute. Then she glanced back at him, her eyes still echoing her need. He reached out a thumb to glide over her swollen lips. Lips he wanted to devour again.

"Want to go out again tomorrow night?" she asked. "I pick the place this time."

Luke looked at her in surprise. Was this another test?

"Okay. Sounds good to me. What time should I pick you up and what should I wear?"

"Eight o'clock and jeans and a T-shirt are fine. Don't overdress. You'll be getting hot."

His body surged to attention at her words. Innocent or not, they were full of innuendo. But she didn't elaborate, so clearly she was going to let him ponder just what it was they were doing.

Chapter Six

Gracie waited inside the door for Luke to come to the steps. He'd seemed bent on coming to get her last night, so she'd waited tonight.

He mounted the steps and knocked lightly. She opened the door and bit back a smile of satisfaction at his double take.

"You look...fantastic," he murmured.

She reached for her jacket and noted his disappointed grimace when she slid it on. "Ready?" she asked.

She grinned smugly all the way to the truck. The top she'd chosen was more suited for warmer weather. The thin straps looped over her shoulders and the built-in shelf made wearing a bra unnecessary. The material molded and cupped her breasts like a lover. Every curve was outlined in vivid detail. She liked to call it her bitch in heat shirt. And where they were going, she planned to work up a sweat.

"So where we going?" Luke asked when they got into the truck.

"Downtown," she said vaguely.

He looked curiously at her but started the engine and drove out of her driveway. Fifteen minutes later, they got off the freeway and headed toward the downtown section.

"Take the next left," she directed.

They turned onto a smaller street and she pointed toward a stop sign.

"Take a right."

She leaned forward in anticipation as she spotted the club. "Here, turn into the parking lot," she directed.

Luke pulled in and parked then cut the engine. He looked over at her. "Rave? We're going to Rave?"

"You don't dance?" she asked innocently.

"I've been known to dance," he said slowly.

"Then let's go."

She slid out of the truck and met Luke around the front. She'd shed her jacket and hopped a bit to keep warm in the cold air.

"Let's get inside before you freeze," Luke muttered.

As soon as they stepped inside, the fast beat of the music swelled and pounded. It vibrated the floor beneath their feet and exploded off the walls. Her pulse quickened as the beat invaded her veins.

"Let's dance," Luke shouted beside her.

He tugged her out toward the crowded dance floor. Couples moved and gyrated in time with the music, their bodies meshed in sensual poses.

Gracie hesitated, unsure of herself for the first time.

Luke leaned in toward her ear. "Pretend for a minute that I'm one of your boyfriends. You've brought me here to dance. Come on, Gracie, what would you do?"

He was taunting her, daring her. And damn it, she never backed down from a dare.

She looped her arms around his neck and swung her pelvis into his groin. She moved and swayed, getting into the heady beat. She closed her eyes and threw her head back as she rubbed her breasts across his chest.

After a few moments, she rotated in his arms, grinding her ass into his hard cock. Oh yeah, she could feel the bulge against her behind. She leaned into him and reached up, twining her arms behind her around his neck.

She writhed against him, bumping and thumping as he moved in sync with her. His hands crept around her, moving slowly, seductively over her belly.

She shivered as a flash of need, centered in her abdomen, shot out in ten directions. Her pussy tightened, her nipples beaded and the hunger within her grew.

His hands moved up inching closer to her breasts. Would he touch her in public? She knew the club goers here were about as uninhibited as they came, but she wasn't sure if Luke would feel comfortable indulging in that sort of activity.

Then he cupped both breasts through the thin material of her shirt and she gasped at the erotic sensation that bolted through her body. He massaged and plumped them both, lightly caressing the sensitive flesh.

One of his hands dropped, sliding down her body as the other kept kneading her breast. Lower still until his thumb brushed over her belt loop and caught there. His fingers dipped to the juncture of her thighs until he touched her pussy through her jeans.

Her body jerked in reaction and she moaned softly. He continued to rub up and down, dipping farther between her legs. She ground her ass against his cock, her movements becoming more restless by the minute.

"Undo your jeans for me," he said close to her ear.

"Here?" she asked.

"This is your place, Gracie. You wouldn't have brought me here if you hadn't wanted this to happen."

She gulped nervously and reached down with shaky fingers to undo the snap of her jeans. Around them, the dancing continued and no one seemed to notice or care what she and Luke were doing.

"Arms back up now," he ordered.

She slid her arms back up over her head and wrapped them around his neck until she was once more locked in his embrace.

The hand he had on her breast lowered to the hem of her shirt. He dipped underneath until his hand came into contact with her bare skin. Then he slid his hand back up toward her breasts until he flicked over her nipple.

The nipple ring dangled and he plucked gently at it.

"Very nice," he said in her ear.

She'd forgotten all about the nipple rings and how he might react to them, but based on his response, he was far from turned off.

He continued to play with the nipple ring as his other hand delved into her pants. She sucked in her breath as his fingers found her clit and began rubbing in a slow, torturous circle.

"I want you to come for me, Gracie. Right here, right now."

Oh God, if he only knew just how close she already was.

He pulled harder at her nipple ring and bent his head to nibble at her neck. His fingers moved faster over her pussy, separating the folds and flicking at the button between them.

Her breathing sped up. Then just as he sank his teeth into her neck, he pulled sharply at the nipple ring and he pinched her clit.

She exploded against him in a rush of heat. She sagged heavily in his arms, and he caught her against him, holding her tightly. Wave after wave of exquisite pleasure poured over her as the music swelled in the background. Her legs shook, and she felt weak all over.

Finally he eased his hand from her pussy. He let his other hand fall from her breast and carefully withdrew it from her shirt. He reached around her with both hands and redid her snap before arranging her shirt for her.

“Maybe we should get a drink now,” he suggested.

She nodded numbly and followed him off the dance floor. They took a table far enough from the dancing and music that they might actually be able to hear each other without shouting.

“What the hell was that?” Gracie asked after they placed their drink order.

Luke fixed her with one hell of a sexy stare. “I should be asking you that. Didn’t you set me up for that?”

She opened her mouth but couldn’t think of a single thing to say. “No, I mean yes, but no, I wasn’t setting you up. I just wanted to see…”

“If I’d run scared if you took me to a place like this?” he finished.

“Yeah,” she finished lamely. “Something like that.”

“I’m not like your other boyfriends, Gracie.”

“No, you’re not,” she said truthfully. “That was, honest to God, the hottest thing that’s ever happened to me in my life.”

Luke grinned. “Honest. Yep, that’s what I love about you.”

“You didn’t…you didn’t mind the nipple rings?”

He stared strangely at her. “Mind? I was turned on as hell. I can’t wait to see them. I bet you look incredibly sexy with them dangling from your nipples.”

She grabbed for the drink being delivered and drank greedily. God, she had to do something to cool off or she was going to go up in flames.

Finally she put it down and stared intently at Luke. “Is that where we’re headed, Luke? Are we going to have sex?”

“I could lie and say no, but I won’t. That’s precisely where we’re headed, Gracie.”

Delicious tickles licked up her spine. Her insides quivered and her nipples tightened. For the first time in a long time, she looked at sex and had no idea what to expect.

“Not right away,” he continued. “I want to see you a few more times. I’m having fun seeing you as more than a buddy. You’re a beautiful woman, Gracie, and I’m enjoying you very much.”

He leaned in toward her until his mouth was inches from hers. “Would you trust me enough to go somewhere with me for the weekend? For Valentine’s Day?”

“Valentine’s Day?” she echoed.

“Call it our fantasy weekend,” he said. “Make plans to get next Friday off work. I’ll pick you up Friday morning, and we’ll spend the weekend together. I promise you won’t regret it.”

She sat back in her chair and stared at him open mouthed. Spend an entire weekend with him. Having sex. A fantasy weekend. Her entire body tingled at the thought.

“Do you trust me?” he asked.

She nodded. “You know I do.”

“Then let me plan this. Say you’ll go.”

She must be out of her mind. No one did this sort of thing after two dates. But this was Luke. Not some schmuck she'd just met. She knew he wouldn't hurt her and would probably give her the best sex of her life.

"Okay," she said. "I'll do it."

"Good. That's just next weekend. Not long at all to wait."

"No," she agreed. "So what do we do in the meantime?"

"We get to know each other better," Luke said. "And we dance some more."

He gestured toward the dance floor. "You ready for round two?"

Chapter Seven

"So what is Jeremy doing for you for Valentine's Day?" Gracie asked as she leaned against Michelle's kitchen counter. She, Ellie Turner and Michelle were all gathered in the kitchen while the men sat in the living room ready to watch the fight.

Michelle stopped stirring the tea and set the pitcher aside. She smiled ruefully. "Nothing romantic I imagine. He'll probably finish painting the baby's room and we'll probably go pick out the crib."

"Sounds exciting," Gracie said dryly. "What about you, Ellie? If I know Jake, he's planned something terrific."

A blush worked its way over the pretty brunette's face. "I don't know exactly," Ellie said. "He told me not to make plans."

Michelle grinned. "Jake does plan the most wonderful surprises."

Gracie nodded. "Lucky bitch. What I wouldn't give for a man to look at me the way Jake looks at you, Ellie." Even as she said it, the memory of the way Luke had stared at her on their date sent a slow burn straight up her spine.

Ellie laughed and blushed again. "I'm not complaining. I'm so lucky to have him."

Michelle reached over and patted her arm. "No, honey, he's lucky to have you."

"No doubt," Gracie agreed. "Who else would put up with all that testosterone?"

"Oh, I don't know, Gracie. You have to admit all that bottled he-man stuff is awfully sexy," Michelle said cheekily.

"I swear those pregnancy hormones are raging. You must keep Jeremy awfully busy," Gracie said dryly.

Michelle blushed. She actually blushed. Gracie crowed in delight. "Busted!"

The three women dissolved into laughter.

"What about you, Gracie? Got any plans with Luke?" Michelle asked pointedly.

Gracie felt her cheeks heat, but damn it, she was not going to betray herself like the other two women. "Yeah, we're spending the weekend together."

Michelle raised one eyebrow. "The weekend as in you'll have a couple of dates or the weekend as in spending every minute together?"

"The latter," Gracie replied.

"Wow, you guys move fast. Going anywhere special?"

"I don't know exactly. He's planning it. I just know it involves sex."

Michelle pinned her with a questioning stare. "You nervous?"

"Of course I am. This isn't just any guy. I don't want to screw things up."

"You'll do fine," Michelle soothed.

"Luke's a great guy," Ellie interjected.

"What are you girls doing in here?" Luke asked as he walked into the kitchen.

"Gossiping, of course," Michelle said lightly.

Luke dropped a kiss on Michelle's cheek. "How are you feeling, sweetheart?"

Michelle smiled at him. "I'm doing good. Baby's growing like a weed."

He turned to Ellie and gave her a quick hug. "What about you? Jake treating you good?"

Ellie's smile lit up her entire face.

"I'll take that as a yes," Luke said.

Then he turned his attention to Gracie.

Gracie felt an odd shiver as Luke reached to pull her into his arms. He kissed her lightly on the lips before pulling away.

"The fight's starting. I wondered if y'all needed help with the snacks," he said.

The girls put it into high gear. Gracie shoved a tray at Luke while Michelle collected the tea pitcher and the bags of chips. Ellie grabbed the glasses of ice and followed everyone else into the living room.

It was a familiar scene. One that brought Gracie comfort. All of them gathered at Jeremy and Michelle's to watch a UFC fight.

"Hey, Gracie, come sit," Wes called. He patted the spot beside him on the couch.

Luke sat down on the floor in front of her and leaned back between her legs so his back rested against the couch. Ellie sat nestled in Jake's arms, and Gracie felt a pang of longing at the couple's obvious devotion.

They spent the evening laughing and having a good time. Luke didn't go out of his way to latch onto her in front of the others, a fact she was grateful for.

She didn't want to flaunt her budding relationship with Luke. She still felt awkward about it and didn't want to extend that discomfort to the rest of the group. And to everyone else's credit, they'd acted completely normal.

The fight had been over a few minutes when the doorbell rang. Jeremy got up and disappeared from the living room to answer it. A few seconds later, he reappeared.

"Gracie, Keith is at the door for you."

Gracie stiffened. Why now of all times? Did he never think to call or at least go by *her* house if he had something he wanted to say? Why he was fond of making a scene in front of her friends, she'd never know.

"Has he been drinking?" Gracie asked as she got up.

Jake's eyebrows shot up, and his face darkened.

Jeremy shook his head. "I don't think so, and he'd be a damn fool to show up here if he had." He winked at her. "I gave him my best cop stare and told him he better not start any shit."

Gracie grinned. "Thanks, Jeremy."

Luke put a hand on her shoulder as she got up from the couch. "I'm going out with you."

She hesitated for a moment then nodded. As they left the living room, Luke slid an arm around her waist and squeezed reassuringly.

When she opened the front door, Keith, who was standing on the porch with his back to her, turned around. His lips curled in distaste and his eyes glinted with a little fear as he spotted Luke.

"What do you want?" Gracie asked.

"I'd hoped we could talk alone," Keith said, looking pointedly at Luke.

Luke pulled her closer up against him, his hand resting possessively on her hip. "Whatever you have to say to Gracie can be said in front of me. Isn't that right, sweetheart?"

"So you're with him now?" Keith demanded.

"It would appear I am," Gracie said calmly.

"Damn it, Gracie. You don't even give a guy a chance," Keith complained. "You can't expect to spring shit on me like you did. I know I reacted badly, but what did you expect?"

Gracie raised her eyebrows. "Expect? I don't guess I expected anything from you at all, Keith. I've said all I intend to say on the matter. We're finished, and I'd really appreciate it if you'd quit coming over to my friends' house."

"So would I," Luke drawled.

Keith ran his hand through his hair and swore again. "All right, Gracie. If that's what you want. Your loss."

He turned and stomped off the front porch toward his truck. He peeled out of the driveway and left in a cloud of dust.

"Dumbass," Gracie muttered.

"What did you ever see in him?" Luke asked as they walked back into the house.

"Don't rub it in."

Luke laughed. "Okay, I'll shut up now."

"Good idea."

"Everything okay, Gracie?" Jeremy asked as she and Luke entered the living room.

"Yeah, he's gone," she said.

"Maybe you and I should pay Keith a little visit in the official capacity," Wes said to Jeremy. "We could tell him to leave Gracie the hell alone."

"Is he bothering her?" Jake asked with a scowl. "Do I need to go beat his scrawny ass?"

"I can take care of myself just fine, Jake," Gracie said. "But thanks. You guys are the best."

"Who wants a beer?" Michelle interrupted.

Gracie looked gratefully at her, and Michelle winked back.

"Who wants to watch the fight again?" Jeremy asked as he picked up the remote.

Chapter Eight

Gracie leaned back in Luke's truck seat and tried to settle her nervous stomach. They were headed out of town to a cabin on the lake Luke and Wes shared ownership in.

She'd been out before. They'd gotten together for fishing trips and stayed weekends at the cabin, but she'd never gone with the idea of having sex with Luke.

The week leading up to the weekend had been terrific. She and Luke had spent every day together. The sexual tension between them had grown into an enormous entity, but more than that, their relationship had developed beyond their casual friendship.

And now they were adding sex to the equation. It seemed so important to him that she trust him. She did. She'd always trusted him, and it felt right for them to be together. Somehow she *knew* Luke would satisfy all her needs and desires.

"You're quiet," Luke said beside her. "Having second thoughts?"

"No, not at all."

She slid her eyes sideways to look at him. The heat in his gaze peeled a few layers of her skin off. No, she had many thoughts, but she wasn't regretting her decision to see where the weekend would take them.

He reached over and curled his hand over hers. “I'm glad. I'm really looking forward to this. To us.”

She smiled. “Me too.”

Thirty minutes later, they pulled up to the cabin overlooking Sam Rayburn Lake, and Luke cut the engine. He turned sideways in his seat and looked intently at her.

“I've planned a lot for us this weekend. If you ever feel uncomfortable with the direction we're going or I'm doing something that you don't want, just say so. I'll stop. Otherwise, I expect you to do exactly as I tell you.”

A full body shiver worked its way over Gracie's skin. She nodded, her mouth too dry for her to speak.

He leaned in and kissed her, his lips working hot over hers. When he pulled away, his eyes were half-lidded, and desire burned brightly, making his eyes a darker blue.

“I want you to go inside to the bedroom. Remove your clothes and lie down on the bed. Wait for me. I'll be in with our bags.”

She swallowed and nodded again.

He handed her the keys, singling out the one to the cabin.

“Just leave them on the coffee table in the living room and head to the bedroom. Our weekend starts now.”

She got out of the truck and headed for the door. She inserted the key into the lock and went inside. Luke had evidently been here in preparation for their weekend. The cabin was warm, and she could hear the hum of the heater. A fire had been laid in the fireplace, just waiting to be lit.

She set the keys down on the coffee table and headed for the bedroom. Once there, she ran her hands up and down the sides of her jeans, trying to work up the courage to do as he'd told her.

Her body tingled from head to toe. Her pussy hummed, warm vibrations swirling between her legs. The anticipation was nearly sending her over the edge.

Knowing she was only stalling, she undid her jeans and peeled them down her legs. She pulled her sweater over her head and tossed it aside. She hesitated for a slight moment before removing her underwear and bra.

Feeling vulnerable standing in the middle of the room—naked—she moved to the bed and crawled onto the warm comforter. She turned over onto her back and waited for Luke.

She heard him moments later and looked over to see him standing in the door.

"You look magnificent."

She smiled and watched as he moved closer to the bed. He sat down on the edge and reached his hand out to smooth over the skin of her belly.

His fingers worked their way up until he fiddled with her nipple rings. Fine little goose bumps broke out over her flesh as he tweaked and plucked at her nipples.

"Are you ready for this, Gracie?"

"Yes," she whispered.

"Get up," he directed.

She climbed off the bed and stood beside him. He circled an arm around her waist and pulled her down to his lap. At first she didn't understand how he was positioning her, but he turned her so she lay across his lap, belly down. Oh God. She knew what this was about.

His hand glided over her back and to the curve of her ass. Then without warning, his palm smacked down, sending a current of fire through her body.

He petted her and soothed the area before slapping the other cheek with his open hand.

She twisted restlessly against him, needing something, not quite sure what. The blows stung, but directly on the heels of the impact came such delicious pleasure. She was at a loss as to how to describe it, how to react to the erotic spanking. He was giving her exactly what she'd said she fantasized about.

Three, four more times his hand met with the plump flesh of her behind. She moaned softly and squirmed even more.

Then as suddenly as he'd pulled her down, he stood up, picking her up with him.

"Stand right here and don't move," he said as he positioned her by the bed.

In a few seconds he returned with a piece of rope. She trembled as he pulled her hands behind her back and began coiling the rope around her wrists. When he finished, he pushed her gently toward the bed.

"Lay face down on the bed, feet on the floor."

She bent over the bed, placing her cheek against the mattress, and planted her feet on the floor. Her ass was vulnerable and exposed in this position, and it made her even wetter.

She heard him walk away then return. Smooth wood made contact with her ass with a crack that made her jump. She closed her eyes and tensed, waiting for the next blow.

Another followed close behind and then another. Her ass was on fire, the tingling nearly painful in its intensity. She needed release, needed to come, but she was helpless to his demands.

"I want to fuck you so bad, right here, right now," Luke said behind her. "Your ass is so red, so sensitive."

She moaned again as the paddle came down across her butt. “Please,” she whispered.

She heard the sound of a zipper and knew he had undone his jeans. Then she heard the crinkle of a wrapper and before she could process anything further, his hands gripped her thighs, spreading her, and in one motion he plunged into her pussy.

She cried out at the almost unbearable fullness. He hadn’t taken off his jeans, merely unzipped them enough to get his cock free. She could feel the scratch of denim against the tender skin of her ass. She wasn’t going to last long.

He began pumping in and out of her, and she was trapped beneath him, unable to move, only able to accommodate his thrusts. She strained against her bonds, needing to be free but delighting in the sensation of being bound, subject to his mercy.

Her orgasm built and spread, preparing to explode. With each thrust, the pressure in her belly grew until she bucked against him, desperate for release.

He wrapped his big hands around her waist and pulled her back to meet each thrust. He leaned into her, pressing her further into the bed, his weight pushing his cock even deeper.

“Luke!” she cried out.

Just as she felt him pick up his pace, her orgasm burst upon her with the speed of an explosion. She tried to scream but no sound came out. She had a mouthful of the bedspread, her teeth dug in with the agony of her release.

Every muscle in her body tensed painfully as Luke rocked her body against the bed. He strained against her, holding himself deep as his hips spasmed.

“God, Gracie,” he gasped out as he shuddered again.

She went limp underneath him, and he collapsed against her back, his ragged breathing close to her ear. He felt good, his big body covering hers, his cock still wedged deep into her pussy. When he finally moved, she made a sound of protest.

He stepped away for a moment then returned and began untying her hands. When she was free, he climbed onto the bed and pulled her up into his arms.

She cuddled into his chest and rubbed her cheek against his shirt.

“No fair, you’re still dressed.”

He laughed. “I won’t be for long. That was incredible, Gracie. Thank God I brought so many condoms. I think we’re going to need every last one of them.”

He wrapped his arms tighter around her and held her close as they rested.

“It was perfect,” she whispered. And it had been. It was as if he’d reached into her mind and plucked out every exacting detail of what she wanted from a man.

He bent to kiss her. “I’m glad. But we’re only getting started.”

Chapter Nine

Gracie lay cuddled in Luke's arms for a long moment. Finally, he pulled away from her and stood beside the bed. He began shedding his clothing, and Gracie stared with unabashed admiration.

His body was beautiful. There was no other way to describe it. Tight, well muscled, the dips and contours were meant for exploring. She couldn't wait.

As he pulled his jeans off, his semi-erect cock flashed in her view. She ached to reach out and touch it. She wanted to fondle it and stroke it, watch it spring to life under her attention.

He was built for a woman's pleasure. There wasn't a woman alive who wouldn't want a cock this size and wouldn't die of pleasure in the process.

"Do you like what you see?" Luke asked as he stood before her.

She licked her lips. "I want to taste you," she said.

Luke groaned. "Damn, Gracie, you make me crazy."

He got back onto the bed and settled over her body. He lowered his mouth to hers, nipping and sucking at her bottom lip. His lips traveled down the line of her jaw to her neck and then around to her chest.

"I've been dying to taste your nipples," he said hoarsely as he closed his mouth around one.

She arched into him, moaning at the sweet pleasure that streaked from her breasts to her abdomen.

He caught the ring between his teeth and tugged gently. He swirled his tongue around the stiff peak before capturing it between his teeth and nibbling delicately at it.

She worked her hands into his hair and held tightly to him as he sucked at her nipples. He feasted on the sensitive buds, licking, sucking, and biting.

Finally he kissed his way to her belly. He ran his tongue around her navel, leaving a wet trail as he moved lower.

He tugged her legs apart as he moved his body down the bed. Her pussy throbbed in anticipation. He gently parted the slick folds with his fingers then bent his head to lick her clitoris.

Her body jerked in reaction, and she sighed in absolute pleasure. His fingers worked lower, sliding into her opening as he nibbled and licked at the quivering bud.

She closed her eyes and surrendered herself completely to what he gave her. Already she could feel her nerve endings tightening, the familiar rise to something wonderful.

He spread her legs wider and moved off the bed long enough to slip on another condom. Then he slid up her body, settling between her legs.

He played with her nipple rings as his cock nudged at her pussy entrance. He bent and nipped sharply at the quivering peak just as he thrust into her.

As his hips bucked forward, he gathered her in his arms, holding her tightly as he slid into her. His lips moved hotly over her neck and to her mouth, capturing her in a breathless kiss.

He moved powerfully between her legs, stroking to her deepest regions. He felt so big. He stretched her, the friction caused by each thrust making her mindless. She grabbed at his shoulders, sinking her nails deep.

His hands slid down her body until he grasped her buttocks. He squeezed and kneaded as he cupped her against his body. He spread her wider, diving impossibly deep into her. Then he trailed one hand between them, finding her clit and pinching it between his fingers.

She bolted upward, straining against him as he stroked the quivering flesh. He thrust again and again until she panted beneath him.

Her orgasm built to impossible heights and still she hung there, creeping ever closer but not tumbling over the edge. She clamped her teeth together and squeezed her eyes shut as the pressure became nearly unbearable.

He began rocking into her, faster, his thrusts harder. He set an impossible pace and demanded her body keep up.

"Oh God, oh God," she chanted as she felt her body began to splinter apart.

She let out a long wail as he slammed into her again. Around her the room blurred and she felt a thousand strings break in her pussy.

He moved frantically against her, his orgasm racing over him as she found her own. Sweat dripped from his forehead as he arched into her one last time.

She went limp a second before he collapsed over her. It took all her energy but she wrapped her arms around him and held him close as he fought to catch his breath.

"Are you all right?" he rasped in her ear.

"Mmmm hmmm." It was all she could manage.

He rolled to the side and discarded the condom before rolling back over to pull her against him.

"Rest, sweetheart. I'll get up and fix us something to eat in a little while."

She curled into him, feeling ridiculously content. He stroked her hair as her eyes fluttered and closed.

Gracie awoke to find Luke standing over the bed. He bent and smoothed her hair away with his hands then kissed her.

"Time to eat," he murmured.

She stretched and slid out of bed. Luke caught her against him and stroked his hands over her naked skin.

"You better get dressed or I'll never eat," he said.

She grinned and reached for her shirt.

As she followed him into the kitchen, she sniffed appreciatively. Then she saw what he'd cooked.

"Oh my God, you made barbeque chicken!"

He smiled and gestured for her to sit down.

She took her seat, and Luke took the chair across the table from her. She dug in with her fork, uttering a contented sigh when the chicken hit her tongue.

"Are you okay with things so far?" he asked.

She paused, setting her fork down on her plate. "Yeah, and you?"

"I just had the best sex of my life. I'd say that qualifies as okay," he said dryly.

Familiar heat flooded her cheeks.

"If you don't stop looking at me like that, you're not going to be able to finish eating," he warned.

She ducked her head but smiled at the desire in his voice.

When they finished eating, Gracie started toward the sink to put her plate up, but Luke intercepted her.

"You go wait for me in the bedroom. I want you on your knees on the rug. Naked. Hands behind your back."

She swallowed nervously even as a thrill shot down her spine. She nodded and handed the plate to Luke. Her legs shook as she walked toward the bedroom.

She only paused a moment before shedding her shirt. Then she walked over to the plush rug that covered the floor in front of the bed and sank to her knees.

Rising up slightly, she put her hands behind her so they were clasped in the small of her back. Streaks of need pulsated and radiated from her pussy into her abdomen as she imagined what Luke would do when he came in.

She didn't have to wait long. He strode into the room, naked. He stopped when he saw her, his eyes darkening with approval and lust. His cock sprang to attention, and Gracie enjoyed a moment of triumph that she affected him so.

"Do you have any idea how sexy you are?" he asked.

He stopped in front of her and reached out to thrust his hand into her hair. He palmed the back of her head, cradling it as he directed his cock at her mouth.

"Take me deep," he commanded.

She opened her mouth, and he thrust to the back of her throat. He rocked his hips back and forth as she swallowed and sucked at him. He gripped her head, holding her tightly against him.

He pumped into her mouth for several seconds before finally easing from her lips. He reached down and pulled her up to stand in front of him.

He fiddled with her nipple rings, pulling them until her nipples stretched in front of her. "I love these," he said. "They're sexy. Like you."

She twisted, jittery and needy as he plucked at her nipples. She was hot and restless, ready to see what he had in store for her next.

His fingers trailed down her body, over her belly and lower to her pussy. He dipped a finger between her legs, sliding into her wetness. Her knees shook and threatened to buckle.

"Get on the bed," he ordered. "Belly down, legs apart."

She did as he directed, crawling onto the mattress and lying down until her cheek met with the comforter. She spread her legs and stretched her arms above her head.

He crawled between her legs, pressing his chest against her back. He nudged her thighs farther apart with his knee then positioned his cock at her pussy opening.

He surged forward, pressing her further into the bed. His body covered her and his hips dug into her ass as he plunged deeper.

He reached above her, holding her wrists with his hands. She was unable to move as he thrust between her legs. Finally he let her arms go and dropped his hands down to her ass. He squeezed and massaged, pushing upward to gain better access to her pussy.

Then he began thrusting in earnest, increasing his pace until the force pushed her up the bed. He bent down and nipped sharply at her neck until goose bumps dotted her back.

The throbbing between her legs bloomed and spread outward, radiating to every sensitive region of her body. She loved this dominant side of him, loved that he never once stopped to ask her what she wanted or if what he was doing was okay.

She panted as he rocked against her. She was so close and yet she couldn't get there. Her orgasm built and built until it was painful in its intensity.

He grasped her hips with both hands, pushed up so her body angled to give him better entry, and he plunged home. She let out a wail as her orgasm cracked and burst around her. It hurt, it pulsed, it was the most exquisite form of torture she'd ever endured.

And it went on and on.

He collapsed forward, coming to rest at the deepest point in her pussy. His chest pressed into her back, and his body melded to hers. A perfect fit.

She arched her ass into his pelvis, not wanting him to leave her just yet. They both heaved as they tried to catch their breath. Finally, he rolled off her, and she immediately felt cold without him covering her.

She mewled softly in protest, and he gathered her in his arms, once again wrapping his body around hers. He kissed her softly.

"Go to sleep, Gracie. I'll be here. I'm not letting you go."

Chapter Ten

Gracie woke to the sun shining in the bedroom window. The space beside her was empty, and she smelled bacon cooking. She smiled. Luke must be in the kitchen cooking breakfast.

She stretched and climbed lazily out of bed. Luke's flannel shirt lay in a heap on the floor, and she reached for it. She slipped it on, leaving it unbuttoned down the front. His scent surrounded her, and she wrapped the shirt tighter around her.

She padded barefoot out of the bedroom toward the kitchen, a wicked smile on her face. She'd tease him with a few glimpses of those nipple rings he loved so much. By the time breakfast was done, he'd be a walking hard-on.

She rounded the corner, letting her shirt gape a bit wider and let out a squeak of surprise. She yanked her shirt closed and stared at Wes who was standing in the kitchen leaning against the countertop.

She started to back up but Wes closed the distance between them.

"I-I didn't know you were here," she sputtered.

She gripped her shirt even tighter, sure her face was as red as a stoplight. To her surprise, Luke stood by the stove, his expression one of interest as he watched her.

Wes stopped in front of her and reached down for her hand. He tugged her forward into the kitchen.

"Come on now, Gracie," he drawled. "You've seen me naked. Time for me to return the favor."

She shivered slightly under his intense stare. "Is this a practical joke or something?"

Wes ran his hand up the lapel of her shirt, nudging it slightly aside until her breasts peeked around the edge.

"No joke. We've been friends a long time, Gracie. I don't want to make you uncomfortable, but I don't think you are. I think you're as turned on as I am right now."

She cocked her head in confusion and shot Luke a panicked look.

"Quit dicking with her," Luke said.

"You want a threesome," Wes said. "Luke and I want to give you one."

Her mouth rounded to an O and her eyes widened. Wes' fingers brushed across her nipples, flicking lightly at the rings.

She looked back over at Luke again to see him staring intently at her.

"If you don't want this, just say so," Luke said quietly. "We don't want to do anything to make you uncomfortable."

"Wow," she whispered. "I mean, I don't know what else to say. You're okay with this?" she asked Luke.

He smiled. "Who do you think invited Wes?"

"Holy shit." She shook her head, unsure of whether or not she was dreaming. A threesome. Not with strangers. With two men she trusted implicitly. Two men who cared for her and would make it good. Not much to think about there.

"What do you say, Gracie?" Wes murmured.

She nodded. "Okay."

Wes nudged her chin up with his knuckle, and she looked into his warm brown eyes.

"I don't want things to be awkward for us. We've been friends too long for that."

He leaned in and brushed his lips across hers. His goatee rubbed softly on her chin. Bubbles of excitement took flight in her chest. She relaxed against him, and he deepened the kiss.

Her shirt parted as his hands slid underneath the material and cupped her breasts. His thumbs worked over her nipples, and his hands moved down her skin.

Shedding her inhibitions, she wrapped her arms around his neck and kissed him back, letting her tongue roam playfully over his.

It was a different experience kissing Wes. He was more gentle than Luke but every bit as sensual. If she gave herself time to analyze the situation, she'd likely retreat in mortification, but it felt right.

Wes wrapped his hands around her waist and hoisted her upward until she sat on the countertop.

"Much better," he murmured.

Her breasts were now level with his mouth, and he took advantage. His tongue rubbed lightly over one nipple. It puckered and her muscles tightened in response.

He cupped her breasts with both hands and held them up for his mouth to devour.

"I never knew you had such a wild side, Gracie. I like it. The rings are hot."

She moaned as he sucked her nipple into his mouth, his tongue toying with the ring.

"She needs to eat," Luke interjected.

Wes slowly pulled away, and it was all Gracie could do not to insist she wasn't hungry so they'd take her to bed. Her stomach contradicted her by rumbling.

Wes lifted her down as Luke set a plate on the table for her. She walked unsteadily to her chair and sank down into it. She pulled her shirt tight around her, suddenly giving up the idea of making Luke crazy. He'd completely turned the tables on her.

The two men sat down on either side of her and proceeded to polish off their plates of food. She managed to nibble down a small amount, but her stomach was in full somersault mode, and she knew she wouldn't do much justice to her food.

"If you're done picking at that, I know something we could be doing that's a whole lot more fun," Wes spoke up.

She flushed and pushed her plate away. Wes held out a hand to her and pulled her from her chair. Luke walked toward the bedroom, and Wes swung her into his arms and followed.

Wes deposited her on the bed, her shirt falling open She quickly pulled her shirt off and tossed it off the bed. Wes and Luke stepped back and began stripping out of their clothing. She watched, not missing a single detail.

Her heart beat a little faster as Wes moved toward the bed. His cock was impressive. A size that would make a woman stand up and pay attention. It brought to mind all sorts of yummy questions. Would it fit? How delicious would it feel to accommodate all of him?

Wes grabbed her ankles and pulled her toward the edge of the bed. Her legs fell open, baring her pussy to him. He made a sound of appreciation as he bent his head.

Just the anticipation of him touching her with his mouth had her ready to burst. When his tongue finally rubbed over her delicate folds, she nearly came on the spot.

"You taste as good as you look, Gracie," he said. "Sweet."

She arched her back and moaned as his tongue delved deeper. The bed dipped and swayed as Luke climbed up beside her. He bent his head to her breasts, and she cried out as both men tormented her with their mouths.

Wes slid a finger into her pussy. "God, you're so tight, Gracie. I don't want to hurt you."

He left her for a brief moment then his finger slid back into her, gliding easily inside. He smoothed lubricant into her, easing his fingers around the walls of her pussy.

She heard the crackle of a condom wrapper and the sound of more lubricant being squeezed out. Then the head of his cock butted gently against her entrance.

Luke moved from her breasts to her lips, kissing and sucking at her mouth. His hands feathered over her nipples, tweaking and pinching at the taut peaks.

Wes slid easily into her, and she gasped at the fullness. He came to rest deeply within her, and she struggled to process the bombardment of sensations.

"Am I hurting you?" Wes rasped.

"God no," she managed to get out.

Never before had she felt this way. Wes was seated deep within her pussy while Luke kissed her, toyed with her breasts. It was the most exquisite pleasure, every one of her most sensitive spots being teased and touched.

Wes began to move, gently at first and then with more force as she arched her hips to meet his thrusts. Her tongue tangled with Luke's, and she wrapped her arms around his neck, holding him close to her.

Wes pulled away from her and ran his hands over her legs. "Turn over on your hands and knees," he said.

She scrambled over, allowing Wes to position her to his liking. Luke sprawled out in front of her, his cock in perfect position for her to bend down and take it in her mouth.

Gentle hands spread her thighs then Wes mounted her, sliding into her from behind. She closed her eyes and moaned. Luke smoothed her hair from her face as she rocked back against Wes. God, it felt good.

She opened her eyes then slowly lowered her mouth, letting her tongue slide over Luke's hard cock. His hand tangled in her hair, and he groaned as her mouth closed around the head.

So far the reality of a threesome far surpassed her lame fantasies. Being between two men, their focus solely on her, their hands and bodies touching and pleasing her, it was a ride on the most exhilarating roller coaster.

"Gracie, honey, you drive me crazy," Wes said in an agonized voice. "You're so tight, so beautiful."

"Very beautiful," Luke murmured below her.

Luke stroked her hair, running his fingers through the strands as she sucked his cock.

"We want to take you at the same time, Gracie. Are you up for that?" Luke asked.

She shuddered, her orgasm lurking so close. Just the image of them both buried in her body had her teetering on the edge.

Wes withdrew, and Luke gently pulled her away from his rigid cock. Then Wes moved to the side of her and lay down on the bed, his legs hanging over the edge and his feet planted on the floor.

He reached for Gracie, his big hands positioning her over his cock. "Ride me, Gracie."

She let out a moan as she slowly lowered her body onto his erection. He slid in, the friction nearly unbearable. God, he was so big, she didn't know how Luke would accomplish the feat of taking her too.

"Just relax, sweetheart," Luke said as he ran his hands over her ass.

She felt the cool shock of the lubricant over the seam of her ass and flinched as Luke slid one finger inside. Wes played with her nipple rings as she held herself still on his cock.

"We're going to take this slow and easy," Luke said. "I won't hurt you, Gracie, I swear it."

"I trust you," she whispered.

He eased more lubricant inside her, stretching her slightly with his fingers. After several minutes of stroking and preparing her, he positioned his dick at her tight opening.

"Breathe deep," Wes said. "Breathe in and relax. That's it, baby."

Wes' fingers found her nipples again, pinching and plucking at them, distracting her from the burning and stretching of her ass.

She gasped as the muscle gave way and Luke penetrated her anus. He stopped and gave her time to adjust before slowly moving forward again. He inched his way into her until finally, she felt his hips press into the flesh of her buttocks.

Both men were fully sheathed within her body. She began to shake uncontrollably.

"Easy, sweetheart," Luke soothed. "Make it last. Make it good."

She leaned forward in Wes' arms, letting him support her weight as Luke began to move inside her. Soon they found a rhythm, moving in unison. They both pressed forward, filling her, stretching her, bringing her unbelievable pleasure.

How she managed to accommodate them both, she'd never know, but she'd never enjoyed herself more than at this moment.

"Are you all right?" Wes whispered close to her ear.

"Very all right," she replied. She nipped his ear, and he groaned in response.

Wes' hands slid down her waist, gripping her hips. Luke's hands grasped her shoulders, and they held her against them, captive to their embrace.

"I can't last any longer," she gasped. She fought against the rising tidal wave, but knew she only had seconds.

"That's good because I can't either," Wes said. "Let yourself go, we've got you."

Luke surged forward, burying himself in her deepest regions. Wes bucked upward until she gasped at the pleasure/pain of his penetration.

"Oh God!" she cried.

Her body began to spin out of control. Her vision blurred and she writhed between them, unable to bear the pressure building within her. She erupted with such force that Wes slid out of her.

He grasped her waist with one hand while he used his other hand to position himself between her legs once more.

The two men rocked against her, each straining with their own release.

She screamed. She couldn't help it. She'd never ever had such a powerful orgasm, and it scared and thrilled her all at the same time.

She fell forward onto Wes' chest, and he wrapped his arms around her, holding her and soothing her as she fought to catch her breath.

Luke surged against her ass, pressing her harder onto Wes. He slumped against her for a few seconds before easing out of her and rolling to the side.

She lay panting on Wes. She couldn't move, couldn't speak even if she wanted to. His hands slid gently up and down her back, and he kissed the curve of her neck.

"You are one incredible woman, Gracie."

"That she is," Luke agreed. "I may never walk again after this weekend."

Wes rolled Gracie to the side, still cradled in his arms. He pulled out of her and started to sit up.

"Let me get cleaned up, and I'll be right back."

As Wes got up to discard the condom, Luke pulled her into his arms and tucked her head under his chin.

"Was that good?" he asked.

She stretched and yawned like a contented cat. "I'm not sure I could deal with it if it got any better. Thank you, Luke. I don't even know what to say. That was fantastic. I can't believe you went to so much trouble to make my fantasies real."

"Trouble? More like my pleasure," he said. "You're an incredible woman, Gracie."

Wes climbed on the other side of her and scooted in close. He pressed a kiss to her shoulder and slid his hand down the curve of her waist.

"Rest up, Gracie girl, and we'll do it all over again."

Chapter Eleven

Gracie lay in bed between Luke and Wes and stared up at the ceiling. The euphoria around her had yet to dissipate. Her body still felt tingly and alive on the heels of the most fantastic sex of her life.

She glanced over at Luke, unable to control the softening in her chest. The past week with him had been unbelievable. He'd taken their conversations and pieced together her fantasies. He'd made them come alive, and he'd done it because he cared for her.

She wasn't sure exactly when she'd fallen in love with him. In retrospect, she couldn't remember a time when she hadn't felt deeply for him. But the past week had brought it together and shoved it to the forefront. She wanted to be with him.

As if feeling her gaze, he turned his head toward her, his blue eyes glowing with contentment. He reached out a hand to cup her cheek.

"I thought I'd light a fire in the fireplace," he said.

She nuzzled her cheek into his palm. "Hmmm, I'd like that."

"Give me five minutes and I'll be back for you."

She watched as he got up and pulled his underwear on. Then he disappeared out of the bedroom.

A warm hand slid over the curve of her hip, over her belly and up to cup one of her breasts. She closed her eyes, enjoying Wes' caresses.

He nibbled lightly at the curve of her neck as he fingered her nipples.

"Did I hurt you earlier?" he asked. "I worried I was too big for you."

She smiled and turned over in his arms. "You won't find me complaining about your dick size," she teased. "I thought I'd died and gone to heaven."

He kissed her lightly, and she felt the penis in question stir to life against her stomach.

"I can't wait to taste it," she said in a sultry voice.

"Shit," Wes muttered. "I can't wait either."

"We have about three minutes before Luke is coming back to get me," she said wickedly. She slid her body farther down the bed until her mouth was even with his erection.

This was the first time she'd gotten this close, and her eyes widened in appreciation. The man was stacked. She licked her lips in anticipation, and Wes flinched beside her.

"God, woman, quit teasing me."

She laughed huskily and lapped her tongue over the head. He flinched again and dug his hands into her hair. She slid her mouth over him, sucking him deep.

"Oh yeah, baby, suck it. Just like that. Damn."

She took him as deep as she could, and his breath left him in one long hiss. She pushed him over onto his back and knelt over his hips, shoving her hair out of the way.

She wrapped her fist around the base of his cock and moved her hand up and down with the motion of her mouth.

"Stop," he moaned. "Baby, stop before I come."

He pulled gently at her hair until he was free of her mouth. His chest heaved with exertion, and his eyes glittered brightly as he stared at her.

"Fire's built," Luke said from the doorway.

She turned to see him leaning against the doorframe, watching her and Wes. She uncurled her legs and stood up beside the bed. Wes got up as well, and they walked out of the bedroom into the living room.

She curled onto the couch directly in front of the fireplace and sighed in pleasure. To her surprise, Luke sat down beside her and pushed her chest down to the cushions. He pulled her arms behind her back and tied them with the same rope he'd used the previous night.

"Totally and completely at our mercy," he murmured.

She closed her eyes and clenched her teeth against the tide of desire rolling over her body.

Luke stood up and pulled her up to stand beside him. He guided her around to the side of the couch then bent her, belly down, over the arm of the sofa. Her feet left the floor, and her cheek rested against the soft material of the couch. Her ass was in the air, vulnerable.

She heard the jingle—of a belt? Seconds later, she felt the sting of leather across her buttocks. She gasped and squirmed. She had no idea who was administering the spanking.

Again the slap of the belt, the sound of it striking flesh, the delicious burn across her ass. After the fourth stroke, she panted for breath. After the fifth and six, she was begging. After the seventh, she felt hands smooth over her burning ass. Fingers curled roughly around her thighs and spread them.

A cock nudged then rammed into her. Wes. Oh God. He wasn't as gentle as he'd been earlier. Maybe he knew now she could accommodate his size. He thrust hard, sending her spiraling into a world of unbelievable pleasure and the thrill of erotic pain.

He paused for a moment, so tightly wedged into her that she couldn't move if she wanted. Then he forced himself deeper and she cried out.

He slipped from her body, and Luke slid into her, immediately replacing Wes. He squeezed and kneaded her ass cheeks as he thrust into her again and again. Then he slapped her butt with his hand, and she yelped. The skin, so sensitive from the belt, tingled and singed under his hand. He rode her harder, spurred on by her cries. His hand rained down again and again until she sobbed her release. And still he continued.

Unbelievably, her body reacted to his demands. She felt herself climb toward another orgasm even as tears streaked down her cheeks from the first.

Then Luke stopped. He smacked her ass one more time before pulling out.

"No!" she cried out. They couldn't stop now. Not when she was so close again.

She heard a chuckle and wasn't sure who it came from. Then she felt her ass being spread, the cool lubricant soothing over her anus. She trembled from head to toe. Wes stepped between her legs. She recognized his touch. Oh God, surely he wasn't going to take her ass.

"We're going to take this nice and slow, Gracie girl," Wes said soothingly. "You're going to take all of me."

She closed her eyes as he positioned his cock and pushed forward. Slowly, the pressure agonizing. Pleasure ripped through her abdomen even as the pinch of pain unsettled her. It was a heady combination.

The couch dipped and Luke picked up her head and slid underneath her. He fisted his cock in his hand and curled his other hand into her hair. He slipped his cock between her lips just as Wes plunged into her ass.

The momentum carried her forward, forcing Luke's dick deep into her mouth. The tightness in her ass was nearly unbearable. Then Wes smacked her cheek with his hand and she bucked against him.

"I'm going to ride you now, Gracie," Wes said as he began moving within her. "I'm going to ride your ass while Luke fucks your pretty mouth."

Gracie closed her eyes, her body tightening and spasming uncontrollably at Wes' erotic language. She was wild with need. She wanted more. She was helpless between them, unable to move. Her body was theirs to do with what they wanted, and she loved it.

They fucked her mouth and her ass, foregoing their earlier gentle style. This was raw sex, hard, sweaty, the kind she'd dreamed about. They were unrelenting as they made demands of her body. They owned her, they used her, and she never wanted it to stop.

She cried out, but Luke thrust deeply into her mouth, halting all attempt at making sound. She closed her eyes, squeezed them tightly shut as her body splintered and broke apart under their relentless assault.

The wet, sucking sounds of their fucking filled the room. Luke's hand wound tightly in her hair, pulling her head closer to his groin. Then Wes grunted behind her and let out a shout as he came.

"Swallow it, Gracie," Luke murmured. "I want you to swallow it all."

He moaned and jerked against the back of her throat then flooded her mouth with his cum. She sucked greedily, wanting to please him in a way she'd never wanted to please a man.

Wes carefully withdrew from her quivering body as Luke finished in her mouth. Wes reached over to untie her hands, and Luke pulled her into his arms.

She lay on his chest, eyes closed, too worn out to form a coherent thought. Luke hugged her closer as he stood, lifting her with him. He carried her into the bathroom and started the shower.

He washed her gently, taking care with the tender parts of her body. When he was finished, he wrapped her in a towel and carried her to bed.

She burrowed into his chest and was vaguely aware of Wes spooning against her back. Gentle hands soothed over her skin, petting and caressing her. She yawned and allowed herself to drift away.

Chapter Twelve

Gracie opened her eyes, a smile on her face. She sighed and snuggled a little deeper into the covers. It was dark outside, so she'd been sleeping for several hours at least. The guys were gone. Probably in the kitchen since they seemed so determined to take care of her this weekend.

She kicked off the covers and flexed her toes. Lord, but she was sore. Deliciously so. Her body felt heavy and languid, the kind of feeling you could only get from deep-seated contentment.

She pulled on her jeans and her sweater, not bothering with a bra. Chances were she wouldn't have her clothes on long enough to worry about anyway.

She walked out of the bedroom and headed for the kitchen. She could hear the guys talking in low voices and smiled. As she got closer, she stopped in her tracks. She kept out of sight and listened to the conversation unfold in the kitchen.

"I have to admit, when you came up with this idea, I was skeptical," Wes said. "I wondered if you'd really heard Gracie right."

Gracie wrinkled her brow. What on earth was he talking about?

"You don't think that now, though," Luke said with a laugh.

Wes chuckled. "Hell no. It's obvious she really wanted this. It's too bad you didn't overhear her a lot sooner."

"I doubt she and Michelle discuss it that much," Luke said. "Gracie's a private person. If she hadn't just broken up with dipshit, I doubt she would have said anything at all."

"You're probably right. Still, it worked out great. You were able to set up this entire weekend, and I think she really enjoyed it."

Luke laughed again. "See, there are advantages to eavesdropping. Gracie would kill me if she knew I'd listened to her conversation, but it worked out great in the end."

Gracie's mouth fell open and a wave of humiliation rolled over her with the speed of a Mack truck. She could barely process what the conversation meant. She was too busy trying to control the burning in her cheeks.

The whole thing had been an elaborate set-up because Luke had overheard her talking to Michelle about her fantasies?

She didn't even realize she'd stumbled into the kitchen until Wes and Luke looked up at her. Guilt flashed in Luke's eyes, and hurt washed over her again.

"Gracie..." Luke began.

She held a hand up, trying to control the shaking. She'd already made a big enough ass of herself. Oh God, when she remembered all they'd done, she just wanted to bury herself in the ground.

"Is that all this was?" she said in a trembling voice. "Were you two just cashing in on my fantasies? You see a way to have a good time at my expense? You are supposed to be my best *friends*."

"God, Gracie, no, you can't think that," Wes protested.

They both started toward her and she shrank back. Her bottom lip trembled and she bit down, ignoring the pain.

"I thought...I thought this week happened because you cared about me," she said painfully, her gaze focused on Luke. "I feel like such an idiot. Why the games? Why the elaborate charade? Why let me fall in love with you if none of this was real?"

"Gracie, you have to listen to me," Luke said desperately.

She spun away, grabbing the keys from the coffee table.

"Gracie, wait!"

She ignored him and ran from the house as fast as she could. She hurled herself into his truck and locked the doors even as she jammed the key in the ignition.

Luke ran out of the house toward the truck, shouting her name. He tried to open the door as she began to back up.

"Damn it, Gracie, don't go!"

She rammed her bare foot on the accelerator and gunned the engine. When she'd backed far enough out of the drive, she threw it into drive and whipped around.

She raced down the highway, her embarrassment so acute she wanted to curl up and die. If you looked up ass in the dictionary, there had to be a picture of her.

A tear slid down her cheek and she wiped angrily at it. Could she have misread the situation any more? She'd just made the biggest fool of herself ever. With guys she considered her best friends on earth. Guys she couldn't even look in the face anymore.

The forty-five minute drive back home seemed interminable. She'd been stupid to take Luke's truck. She'd be lucky if he didn't have her arrested. But then she'd done a lot of stupid things in the past week.

She drove up to her house and parked Luke's truck next to her car. She left the keys in it, knowing he'd come by looking for it. She went inside long enough to get a pair of shoes and her jacket then she got into her car and took off.

She was being hysterical and unreasonable. She knew that much. She'd carried on like a complete nitwit, but she'd been so humiliated to learn the real reason why Luke had gotten close to her.

She drove with no real sense of direction until she found a quiet, secluded place to park. She needed to calm down, start acting rationally again. Again. Ha. She hadn't acted rationally in months.

Her first mistake was going out with Keith. She'd only compounded that mistake by allowing herself to fall in love with her best friend. Her third mistake had been thinking he had feelings for her beyond those of friendship.

She wasn't going to cry. Even though she felt the sting of tears, she was determined not to give in. She'd already made a big enough ninny of herself.

She sat there, staring at the sky, numb. For several hours. Luke would have his truck back by now. He and Wes would be home, probably wondering what the fuck her problem was.

Emitting a weary sigh, she started the engine and drove slowly toward the main road. She instinctively headed for Michelle's. It was late. Or early depending on your point of view, and she hated to disturb her friend's sleep, but she needed a shoulder to cry on in the worst way. This whole stiff upper lip was getting old fast.

It was nearly four in the morning when she pulled into Michelle's driveway. She turned off the engine and slowly got out. Before she closed the door, she saw Jeremy hurry down the steps and stride across the lawn toward her.

She trudged toward him, and he held his arms open to her. He caught her in a hug and kissed the top of her head.

"We've been worried sick about you, Gracie. Come on in. I'll make you some hot chocolate."

She smiled gratefully at him. "I'm sorry, Jeremy. I didn't mean to worry y'all. Especially not Michelle."

"Luke and Wes are worried too," Jeremy said quietly. "I need to call and let them know you're okay."

Gracie stiffened.

"Gracie, Luke is frantic. He's worried something happened to you. I'm just going to call and tell him you're all right."

She nodded, guilt creeping over her.

Once inside, Michelle hurried over and hugged her tightly. Then she dragged her over to the couch and made her sit down.

"What on earth happened?" Michelle demanded.

Gracie sighed and closed her eyes for a moment. "I made an ass of myself. That's what happened."

Jeremy returned and pressed a hot cup of chocolate into her hands.

"Thanks," she said.

Jeremy sat down on the other side of Gracie and put a comforting hand on her leg. "Tell us what happened, Gracie."

She flushed and set her cup down on the coffee table. "Apparently Luke overheard our conversation," she said to Michelle. "The one about my fantasies."

"Ohhh," Michelle said, her eyes wide.

"And apparently he wanted to fulfill those fantasies for me. He asked me out and we spent the week together. I thought he was interested in *me*. I confided those fantasies in him and he arranged this weekend. Wes was a surprise."

She broke off and ducked her head in embarrassment when Michelle's eyes widened further in shock.

"You mean, you and Luke *and* Wes?"

"Yeah," Gracie muttered.

"You're angry with them for not telling you they knew?" Jeremy asked in a confused voice.

Gracie sighed. "I'm not angry with them," she said quietly. "I'm angry with me. And I'm so humiliated I want to just find a hole to crawl in."

"Oh honey," Michelle said. She reached over and squeezed Gracie's hand. "Why on earth should you be embarrassed?"

"I just wish Luke had been up front. Told me from the beginning that this was about sex. Instead he made me believe...he made me believe he cared about me. He made me fall in love with him," she said miserably. "And all along it was just a game. His heart was in the right place. I know he's never approved of the men I've slept with. He wanted to give me a weekend I'd remember. I understand that."

Michelle wrapped her arms around her and hugged tight.

"I let my mouth get ahead of my brain again, and I basically blurted out that I loved him. Just before I ran like a scalded cat. Now I've got them both mad at me because of a huge misunderstanding. One I perpetuated. I guess in a way, I wanted it to be the truth. I wanted Luke to love me."

"Are you so sure he doesn't?" Jeremy spoke up.

She nodded, tears burning holes in her eyelids. "I heard him and Wes talking. And Luke's never said anything to make me believe he cares for me beyond a friend. I just got wrapped up in the whole going out thing and confused sex with love. You'd think I was twelve years old or something."

She bowed her head as hot tears splashed onto her arm. "I screwed up."

Jeremy gently nudged her chin up with his knuckle until she looked him in the eye. "Don't blame yourself, honey. There are two grown men who are as big a part in this as you are. I don't know what the hell happened, but I don't think we have the full story here."

Gracie leaned forward and hugged Jeremy. "I'm sorry to put you in this position. They're your friends too. I just needed to come by and talk to Michelle."

He hugged her back and stroked her hair soothingly. "You're always welcome here, Gracie. Michelle and I love you. Nothing will change that."

"Of course not," Michelle said firmly.

"I should get home," Gracie said as she pulled away from Jeremy.

"You're not going home in your condition," Jeremy said. "You look exhausted. It's four o'clock in the morning. You can crash on the couch and go home after you've rested."

"I'm too tired to argue," Gracie said.

Michelle stood up. "I'll get you some pillows and a blanket. We'll talk more in the morning when you're feeling better."

"Thanks, Chelle. I don't know what I'd do without you guys."

Michelle hugged her again then hurried toward the closet down the hall. She returned a few minutes later with the linens.

Gracie took them gratefully and made a comfortable spot on the couch. Jeremy and Michelle said their goodnights and disappeared into their bedroom.

Gracie sank wearily onto the couch and pulled the covers up to her chin. *Dummy, dummy, dummy.* She closed her eyes. She was even too tired to further castigate herself.

Chapter Thirteen

Luke pulled up to Jeremy and Michelle's house and parked beside Gracie's car. The sun was just starting to peek over the horizon when he mounted the steps to the front porch.

Before he could knock, Jeremy opened the door and motioned for him to be quiet. He followed Jeremy inside and saw Gracie sound asleep on the couch.

"She's wiped out," Jeremy whispered. "She was pretty upset when she got here."

Luke raked a hand through his hair and swore under his breath. What a mess. His gaze drifted back to Gracie, drinking in her appearance. He'd been so goddamn worried when she'd tore off in his truck. He and Wes had driven the entire way home afraid they'd find her wrecked on the side of the road.

"I'm going back to bed with my wife," Jeremy said. "I don't know what all is going on between you and Gracie, but I know she's hurting."

"Thanks for calling me," Luke said softly.

"No problem. I know how worried you were about her."

Luke watched as Jeremy left the room and then he went to kneel beside the couch where Gracie lay. His chest tightened when he saw the evidence of her tears. Tenderly, he stroked her hair away from her cheek then he leaned forward and kissed her lips.

God, he didn't like to see her hurting. He never had. She had a way of twisting him up on the inside that no other woman had ever managed to do.

He hated to wake her up. God knew she could use the sleep. So could he. But they had to talk. He had to make her understand.

"Gracie," he whispered. "Gracie, sweetheart, wake up."

She stirred, twisting her head slightly, a frown marring her face. Then she opened her gorgeous eyes and looked at him in confusion. Hurt filled her gaze, and he felt like someone sucker-punched him.

"What are you doing here?" she whispered.

He stroked his hand over her face, wanting to touch her, reassure himself that she was really okay.

"We need to talk, Gracie."

She nibbled at her bottom lip then slowly nodded. "I know," she said quietly.

"Will you come with me?" he asked. "I don't want to hash everything out here with Jeremy and Michelle in the next room, and I don't imagine you want to either."

She pushed herself up on her elbow and struggled to sit up. He curled his hands around her waist and helped her upright.

"Okay," she agreed.

He breathed a sigh of relief. He'd overcome the first obstacle. Getting her to listen. Now he just hoped he'd be successful in all he had to convince her of.

She stood up, a little shaky on her feet, and he reached out to steady her, but she stepped away. He collected her jacket and held it open for her.

She walked ahead of him out the door, and he carefully closed it behind them. He hurried for his truck, knowing she'd be cold.

He started the engine and turned the heat on high before backing out of the driveway. They didn't speak as he drove toward his house. He didn't know whether to be grateful she wasn't yelling at him or worried that she was so quiet.

A few minutes later, he parked in his garage and looked over at her. "Come in so we can talk?"

Gracie stared at Luke for a long moment. He did look worried about her, and she hated that she'd acted so stupidly. She was still embarrassed as hell, but she'd just made things worse by running.

She finally nodded and opened the truck door to climb out. Luke waited for her in front of the truck and ushered her inside.

He had a gorgeous house. He'd moved into a spec house he'd built when he started developing the neighborhood. She'd always thought it too big for him, but it would be perfect for a family.

She sighed and directed her thoughts away from a family Luke may or may not have in the future.

Luke guided her into the living room and gestured for her to sit down on the couch. She perched on the edge, just wishing they could get the awkwardness over. She needed to beg forgiveness for being such a dipshit, and maybe, just maybe, they could one day go back to being friends again.

He stood a few feet away, looking uncomfortable. Poor guy probably didn't know what the hell to say in the face of her assumptions. He was probably trying to figure out a way to let her down easy.

She sighed again. “Look, Luke, I’m sorry.”

He looked startled by her apology. He started to speak but she held a hand up. “Let me finish please.

She looked down at her hands and sucked in a few steadying breaths. Then she looked back up at him.

“I overreacted. I know that. And I made some assumptions I had no business making. It’s just that I wish you’d been level with me from the get-go. Just told me what you’d planned. You didn’t have to go through the whole charade of getting close to me. I thought...” She took another deep breath, willing herself not to crack. “I thought you were coming to care for me as more than a friend and that this weekend was a natural progression of that relationship. Silly, I know, but not knowing that you’d overheard my conversation and made plans to surprise me, well, it’s the only conclusion I could draw.”

He stared at her, mouth open. Then his eyes sparked. He was angry. Hell.

He strode over to where she sat on the couch and knelt down in front of her.

“Luke, I—”

“Gracie, shut up,” he said fiercely.

She blinked in surprise.

He blew out his breath in an angry puff then he yanked her to him, kissing her roughly, passionately. She had no time to react, and she was too shocked to do so.

He pulled away from her and collected her hands in his. “Gracie, I love you.”

Her mouth fell open. “But—”

"Not a word," he said, his eyes still flashing angrily. "I swear I don't know where you get some of those fool-headed notions of yours. I'm so tempted to turn you over my knee and spank your ass."

Her cheeks warmed as she remembered him doing precisely that.

"This week has been the best week of my life, Gracie. And you're the reason for that. Yeah, I overheard your conversation with Michelle. And yeah, it made me see you in a new light. It made me realize how much we had in common and how stupid I was for never seeing it, for never asking you out.

"Yes, I wanted to give you a weekend you'd never forget, but I also want to give you a lifetime of those weekends. You and me, tearing up the sheets, eating each other alive. Gracie, when I'm with you, I swear I don't even think straight. The chemistry between us is off the charts. But more than that, you're my best friend. I love you. I think I've always loved you, and I want to spend my life with you. There's no one I have a better time with. No one who understands me like you do.

"I fucked up. I should have told you I heard you and Michelle talking, but honest to God, it never even occurred to me that things could go so terribly wrong. I planned to spend the weekend making all your fantasies come true and then I was going to get down on my knees and beg you to make *mine* come true by marrying me."

Gracie stared at him in shock. Her mouth fell open and tears spilled over onto her cheeks.

"You love me?" she whispered.

"After a speech like that, can you doubt it?" he asked.

She laughed and put her hand up to cup his cheek. "Oh, Luke, I was such an idiot. I was so afraid. I'd fallen so hard for you, and in that moment, I was so afraid you didn't feel the same."

He gathered her in his arms and held on tight. "I'm sorry I hurt you, Gracie. I'd never do anything to hurt you on purpose."

She hugged him back, trying to blink away the tears that streaked down her cheeks. Relief and euphoria like she'd never known rolled through her system.

He pulled slightly away and kissed her. He cupped her face in his hands and kissed her so tenderly, so full of love that it was hard to hold the tears at bay.

"Will you marry me, Gracie?"

"Yes. Yes!"

She threw her arms around him again and peppered his cheek and neck with kisses.

The door leading from the garage to the kitchen slammed and Luke whirled around. Gracie saw Wes standing in the doorway to the living room, concern etched on his face.

"Gracie, are you all right?" he asked anxiously.

She looked at Luke and, at his nod, stood up and walked over to Wes.

"I'm fine, Wes. I'm sorry for blowing up like I did."

"Ah hell, Gracie, no need to apologize."

He walked forward and wrapped his arms around her. He squeezed her tight and stroked a hand through her hair.

"I'm sorry if we hurt you, girl. I'd cut off my right arm before doing anything to hurt you."

He drew away and kissed her warmly on the lips. He let his tongue mingle with hers as his hands stroked up and down her back.

"I hope you don't regret the weekend," he said huskily. "You're one special woman. Luke is a lucky man."

She hugged him again. "He's asked me to marry him."

Wes pulled away from her and grinned. "And you said?"

"Yes, of course."

"Well, hot damn. Congratulations. To both of you."

He put his hand out to Luke then pulled him into a bear hug. "I'm gonna get on out of here and leave you two to sort things out."

He ruffled Gracie's hair. "Love you, girl."

She smiled. "Love you, too, Wes. And I don't regret this weekend."

Fire blazed in his eyes. "I'm glad."

He turned and walked back out to the garage, leaving Luke and Gracie standing there.

Luke pulled her into his arms and rested his cheek on top of her head. "Did you mean it? You'll marry me?"

She smiled into his chest. "Just as soon as I can drag you to the altar."

He loosened his hold on her and stuck his hand into his pocket. "I didn't get you flowers for Valentine's Day, but I hope this will make up for it."

He pulled a small ring box from his pants and held it out to her.

She couldn't breathe.

She opened it with shaky hands and saw a diamond ring nestled against black velvet.

"Oh, Luke, it's beautiful!"

He tugged the ring from its perch and slid it onto her finger. "I love you, Gracie."

She admired her ring for a moment then she looked into his eyes. Brilliant blue eyes that burned with love. Love for her.

"I love you, too," she whispered.

About the Author

To learn more about Maya Banks please visit www.mayabanks.com Send an email to Maya at maya@mayabanks.com.

Look for these titles

Now Available

Maiden Flight—Dragon Knights 1 by Bianca D'Arc

Border Lair—Dragon Knights 2 by Bianca D'Arc

The Ice Dragon—Dragon Knights 3 by Bianca D'Arc

Lords of the Were by Bianca D'Arc

Ladies of the Lair—Dragon Knights 1 & 2 (together in print) by Bianca D'Arc

Seducing Simon by Maya Banks

Colters' Woman by Maya Banks

Understood by Maya Banks

Coming Soon:

Prince of Spies—Dragon Knights 4 by Bianca D'Arc

Hara's Legacy—Resonance Mates 1 by Bianca D'Arc

Undenied by Maya Banks

Brazen by Maya Banks

Discover the Talons Series

5 STEAMY NEW PARANORMAL ROMANCES
TO HOOK YOU IN

Kiss Me Deadly, by Shannon Stacey
King of Prey, by Mandy M. Roth
Firebird, by Jaycee Clark
Caged Desire, by Sydney Somers
Seize the Hunter, by Michelle M. Pillow

AVAILABLE IN EBOOK—COMING SOON IN PRINT!

WWW.SAMHAINPUBLISHING.COM

HOT STUFF

Discover Samhain!

THE HOTTEST NEW PUBLISHER ON THE PLANET

Romance, fantasy, mystery, thriller, mainstream and more—Samhain has more selection, hotter authors, and everything's available in both ebook and print.

Pick your favorite, sit back, and enjoy the ride! Hot stuff indeed.

WWW.SAMHAINPUBLISHING.COM

GET IT NOW

MyBookStoreAndMore.com

GREAT EBOOKS, GREAT DEALS . . . AND MORE!

Don't wait to run to the bookstore down the street, or waste time shopping online at one of the "big boys." Now, all your favorite Samhain authors are all in one place—at MyBookStoreAndMore.com. Stop by today and discover great deals on Samhain—and a whole lot more!

WWW.SAMHAINPUBLISHING.COM

Discover eBooks!

THE FASTEST WAY TO GET THE HOTTEST NAMES

Get your favorite authors on your favorite reader, long before they're out in print! Ebooks from Samhain go wherever you go, and work with whatever you carry—Palm, PDF, Mobi, and more.

WWW.SAMHAINPUBLISHING.COM

Printed in the United States
87499LV00004B/94-105/A